THROW DOWN—OR DIE

Tom wanted to pull his pistol right now and pump bullets into these three cold-eyed assassins.

The Pinkerton men were laughing at him. One of them spoke, with a bite in his voice. "You listen, Sheriff. We're the law just as much as you are."

Tom's face was red, his heart was pounding with anger. "I want you three vultures out of this town. I want you out within half an hour." He was aware he was saying too many words. It would have been smarter to get the posse together first. What made him stop talking was the sudden realization of where the fourth Pinkerton was.

Behind him.

Tom tried to turn, clawing for his .45, but he was too late. There was an explosion of light and noise inside his head, a terrible pain, and then . . . darkness.

SPECIAL PREVIEW!

Turn to the back of this book for an exciting excerpt from the magnificent new series . . .

RAILS WEST!

. . . the grand and epic story of the West's first railroads—and the brave men and women who forged an American dream.

LONG RIDER

★ VENGEANCE VALLEY ★

CLAY DAWSON

DIAMOND BOOKS, NEW YORK

This book is a Diamond original edition,
and has never been previously published.

VENGEANCE VALLEY

A Diamond Book / published by arrangement with
the author

PRINTING HISTORY
Diamond edition / May 1993

ISBN: 1-55773-899-8

Diamond Books are published by The Berkley Publishing Group,
200 Madison Avenue, New York, New York 10016.
The name "DIAMOND" and its logo
are trademarks belonging to Charter Communications, Inc.

PRINTED IN THE UNITED STATES OF AMERICA

10 9 8 7 6 5 4 3 2 1

LONG RIDER

★ VENGEANCE VALLEY ★

CHAPTER ONE

It was good land, conducive to modest farming. The terrain was too broken by nature for big farms, like the ten-thousand-acre monsters in California's immense central valley. Here, a number of small valleys were hemmed in by low hills, rising to mountains farther back. There seemed to be one or two farms to a valley, some looking a little more prosperous than others, but none looking particularly rich, just enough to support a single family comfortably.

The valleys were chained together by a stream which broadened out in the flat places, then contracted into a strong torrent where it cut through the rock barriers that separated the valleys. Railroad tracks more or less followed the path of the stream, slicing through the landscape like an old, shiny scar. Civilization. Farms, a railroad. Altered land.

Gabe had been following the stream from the place where it came down out of distant mountains, many miles away. It irked him that he was also following a rail line. The farms irked him, too. Gabe didn't like farms, didn't like the way they broke up the natural features of the land into neat, artificial checkerboards, a boring procession of geometrical lines, where there had once been the wild, yet ordered beauty of nature. Farmland was land where a man could no longer ride where he wanted to ride; he had to think about Private Property, Permission to Pass. Where there was farmland, a man automatically lost his freedom.

There were still areas that were pretty, areas where the plow had not torn up Mother Earth, perhaps places that were too stony, or too steep, or where no one had as yet taken time to plow or put up fences. Most of the farms he passed by had a new look, as if they had been here only a few years.

Gabe tried to imagine what the land might have looked like before the railroad came. For it was the railroad that always brought with it "progress", if only for the unfortunate fact that the rails made it possible for a tenderfoot to leave the East and arrive in the West just a few days later, protected inside a railway coach. A journey that might have taken weeks or even months before the rails were laid down. A journey that had killed many a man or woman not hardy enough for its dangers. Yet, to a certain type of man, it had been those very dangers that had made the trip worthwhile. And, as a corollary, only the strongest had arrived at journey's end. Now, the land was filling with the weak, the unprepared.

How quickly this country was filling up. Gabe remembered his boyhood, when it had been possible to ride for days without seeing other men, or any sign of man's activities. Then, he had ridden with the Oglala, out on the vast plains to the east, riding as one of them, one among the People. Entire villages had been able to pack up at a whim, take down the lodges, load the travois, and migrate to another uninhabited place in the open, free Western lands. No more. Never again would that be possible. Farms. Ranches. Towns. A plague of men. White men. Greedy men, not content with what the land offered of itself, as the People, the Lakota, had been content. No. These were men, this white race, determined to change the land, impose their will upon it, destroy the earth itself if doing so would bring them more profit. That was the key to understanding this new race. Profit . . . the White Man's god.

Gabe continued to study the landscape. Like most Western land, it had a long dry season. He saw small canals leading away from the stream. Irrigation. Eventual death for the land. Over time, the waters from the river, unlike rainwater, would deposit more and more salt into the soil, and the land would die. He'd read about that. When he'd left the People and gone

East to Boston to live with his grandfather, his mother's father, he'd been fascinated by the old man's library. He'd read and read, intent on understanding the White Man's history, because he knew if he could do that he would understand the White Man's mind, since all men, Oglala or white, are usually the product of the lives and thoughts of their ancestors. In one of those books, about long-vanished civilizations, he'd read how the people of the land of Sumer, that most ancient of civilizations, had used the waters of the Tigris and Euphrates rivers to irrigate the broad grasslands in which they lived, and had managed to turn them into a desert. Four thousand years ago. How long would it take to turn this land into a desert?

Gabe did not stop at any of the farms. In a day or so, when the terrain permitted, he would turn off to the north, into as yet untamed land, where he would be able to hunt his supper and drink water from streams unused by man or his tame animals. He would find a place where there was no memory of the White Man. That is, if this chain of farms ever ended.

From time to time, when Gabe passed close enough to a farm, the inhabitants would come out of their houses, or look up from their work, and watch him. But no one called out, or waved; they merely shaded their eyes and watched him ride on by, happy that he was just passing through. For he was clearly not one of their kind. He was no farmer. He had the appearance of a hunter, a wanderer. They were unsure whether he was a hunter of animals, or a hunter of men. But, in either case, he was not one of them.

What the farmers saw was a tall man, riding a big black stallion. The stranger's clothes were trail clothes, durable, simple, protected from road dust and weather by a long linen duster. He wore a trail-stained slouch hat, which shaded his eyes. Those he passed close enough to saw startling eyes, so pale-gray that they seemed to have no color at all. The deep mahogany hue of his face, that particular color a fair skin takes on after a lifetime of exposure to the sun and wind, made those pale eyes all the more noticeable.

Even when he did not ride close enough to the farms for the people to notice the color and coldness of his eyes, they still knew that he was not one of them. It was the guns. Two rifles, stowed in saddle scabbards, a glimpse of the butt of a revolver protruding past the front of the open duster. They saw a heavily armed man, with his world lashed to the back of his horse, passing through. To do what? To whom?

Before the railroad, this stranger's armament would have passed unnoticed; most men riding through these vast Western lands had been similarly armed, for simple survival. Now, it was a land where the most common weapon was the plow. A weapon aimed at the land itself. Yes, men kept guns in their houses, because this was still the West, but they hoped never to have to use them. The weapons that had won this land had grown alien to their hands.

Gabe was aware of the way these farmers viewed him. It did not bother him at all. Not since he'd been very young had he sought the approval of others. Not since he'd lived with a people whose approval he valued, the Lakota, his comrades, those free warriors of the Plains.

His mind drifted back to the past, filled with images of the hunt, closing in on the buffalo, a line of horsemen racing toward a dark sea of fleeing animals, closing in for the kill, enjoying the sport of it, but also appreciating its seriousness, for if they did not kill buffalo there would be nothing for the People to eat. Babies would starve. The old and weak would die quickly. The strength of a man's arm, his skill with his weapons were all that kept the People alive. But still . . . the thrill of it, riding up alongside a panicked, running buffalo, leaning down to press the muzzle of a rifle against that shaggy dark hide, pull the trigger, feel the recoil, see that animal shudder, veer, then go down. Or, more exciting yet, to ride in close, armed only with a bow or lance, tightening one's thighs against the heat of a pony's body, ready to drive a stone tip into half a ton of running meat. Then, when the hunt was over, the women, crying out in triumph as they came running, knives in hand, ready to cut up the meat their men had killed. Killed for them, for the People.

The sound of a woman's cry jerked Gabe from his reverie. Not the sound of a woman's gladness but of a woman's fear and pain. Gabe looked around quickly. The land was rugged here, one of those points where one valley narrowed, ready to open into the next. He heard the sound again. It was coming from the other side of a rock outcrop. He hesitated. The trail continued on around the outcrop. He could avoid whatever lay on the other side of those rocks simply by riding way off to one side. White Man's trouble lay ahead. But he had been lost too long in his memories, memories of a warrior's duty to the weak and helpless. A woman was crying out. . . .

Gabe rode around the outcrop. The trail widened ahead of him, with a small wood to one side and the stream on the other. To one side of the trail, toward the wood, Gabe saw seven people milling together, four armed men struggling with a man and two women. No, with an elderly couple and a young woman. Gabe noticed that the girl's dress was torn, partially exposing one shoulder. The older woman was on the ground, trying to get up, a bruise evident on one cheek. The older man was trying to push past two of the armed men, who were grinning back over their shoulders as the other two closed in on the girl. She tried to run, but one of the men cut her off, grabbed her, tried to pull her close. The girl, obviously terrified, nevertheless fought back strongly, clawing at the face of the man holding her. The man swore, reared back, then slapped the girl hard. She fell, obviously partially stunned. The man started toward her, cursing.

"Goddamn bitch!" he shouted. "You're gonna get yours!"

Suddenly, the older man—he appeared to Gabe to be about sixty—lunged forward, knocking aside one of the men holding him, and ran full tilt into the man closing in on the girl. His fist came up, slamming into the gunman's face.

"Touch her again and you're dead!" the older man shouted.

But now one of the other men had caught up to him. A fist thudded into the back of the old man's neck, knocking him down. When he tried to sit up, the man he'd hit ran up and kicked him in the head, knocking him onto his back. The gunman clawed for the pistol that rode on his right hip. "You stupid old coot!" he shouted. "I'm gonna kill you for that!"

"No!" the girl screamed, trying to push past two of the men toward the fallen man, but they held her back easily.

"You shouldn't o' been so damned hard to get, bitch," one of them snarled. "Now you're gonna . . . Hey!" The sound of rapidly approaching hoofbeats caused him to turn. "Hey!" he shouted again as he saw a mounted man coming hard at him.

Gabe rode in at a canter, drawing his Winchester from its saddle scabbard as he neared the others. He rode his horse straight into the man who'd been about the shoot the older man. The big black stallion's barrel chest slammed straight into the man, knocking him backward, as if he'd been hit by a slow-moving train. The other three gunmen, whose attention had been focused on the girl, now turned to face this unexpected interruption. "Goddamn!" one of them shouted, dropping his hand toward his holstered pistol.

Gabe slammed the barrel of his rifle against the side of the man's head. Blood spurted, and the man went down. Gabe rode toward another man. Dancing out of the way of the snorting, excited stallion, the man was unable to protect himself from the barrel of Gabe's rifle. He too went down.

The fourth man backed away, reaching for his pistol. Gabe cocked the Winchester's hammer. Holding the rifle with one hand while he steadied the stallion, he aimed the rifle's muzzle directly at the center of the man's chest. "It would please me very much," Gabe said calmly, "if you gave me an excuse to kill you."

So far the gunman had only been aware of large shapes—a charging horse, a big man, and a swinging rifle barrel. Now he found himself looking past the muzzle of the Winchester into a pair of the coldest, most expressionless eyes he'd ever seen, eyes without color or apparent compassion, and he knew that if he moved his hand even an inch closer to the butt of his pistol, this stranger with the terrible eyes would kill him instantly. He froze in place. "Just take it easy, mister," he said around a fear-thickened tongue. "No reason a'tall for us to fight."

Gabe quickly swung down from his horse, on the side away from the man he was facing. The man knew that if he wanted to fight, this was his best chance, but he remembered those eyes, the cold killing light he'd seen there, and he did nothing. One of the other men was less cautious, the man who'd been about to kill the old man. Cursing and glaring at Gabe, he got up and started to move toward him. Gabe moved in fast, hit the man across the face with the butt of his rifle. Instantly he reversed the Winchester, sweeping the muzzle over the four men. "Get on your horses and ride," he said tersely. "Or die where you stand. It's all the same to me."

By now, all four of the men were on their feet. Three of them were bleeding from where Gabe had struck them with his rifle. They were still armed, still capable of fighting back, but they were bullies by nature, not true fighters, and this stranger, with his lean, hard, ready body and those terrible eyes, was quite a different kettle of fish than the elderly couple and the girl they'd been brutalizing.

"Hey . . . no reason ta get all het up," one of the men blurted, wiping blood from the side of his face as he backed away. He looked behind him, to where four horses were standing, near a beat-up old buggy. The three other men followed him, backing away, wanting to run but afraid to present their backs to the rifle. They knew what they would have done if they were the stranger—as soon as an enemy turned away, defenseless, they'd be ready to shoot him in the back.

But no shots came. Reaching their horses, the four gunmen jumped up into the saddles, pulled the annoyed animals' heads around, and raced away. Only when they had gotten two hundred yards away did one turn, the one who'd been about to shoot the old man, and shout back, "I'll remember this, you son of a bitch!"

CHAPTER TWO

Gabe watched until the four men were out of sight. He was aware of sounds behind him, and when he finally turned, he saw the two women bending over the old man, who still lay on the ground. Gabe walked over, looked down. The old man had a bad cut on the side of his head. He was trying to sit up, but he seemed groggy. Gabe wondered if he had a concussion.

The younger woman became aware of his scrutiny. She looked up, straight into his face, her eyes studying him. So far, distracted by the action, he had been unaware of her as a woman, but her eyes reminded him. Impressive eyes, large, dark, but most of all, Gabe was struck by the force behind her gaze. Intelligence, strength, and perhaps something just a little bit wild. "We have to get him home," the girl said. "He needs rest."

Gabe nodded. He'd already noticed the beat-up old buggy. Bending down, he helped the girl get the old man to his feet. Together, each holding the old man by an arm, they walked him toward the buggy, while the other woman walked alongside, looking worriedly at the injured man.

"Ach! You treat me like a sick child!" the old man said.

"And you complain like a sick child, Hans," the older woman snapped back. The concern in her eyes revealed her sharpness of tone to be mostly worry.

They got the old man to the buggy. While helping him inside, the girl's torn dress dropped away from one shoulder, baring her left breast. Before he politely looked away, Gabe had a moment in which to notice that, while it was not a large breast, it was perfectly formed. "Your dress, Naomi," he heard the older woman whisper to the girl.

Naomi. A nice name. Gabe noticed that the girl, while nodding to the other woman, did nothing about her dress until they had the old man, Hans, inside the buggy. Then she casually pulled it back up over her shoulder, although it showed signs of slipping again.

With Hans in back, the two women got up on the buckboard, Naomi driving. Gabe mounted, stood watching as Naomi expertly turned the horses, then started them along the stream, in the direction in which Gabe had been riding. He shrugged and called out to the girl, "I'll ride along. Make sure those men aren't waiting for you."

The girl looked up at him as he cantered alongside. Once again, he was aware of something quite remarkable watching him through those dark eyes. "You've done so much already," she said. "You could bring a lot of trouble on yourself. . . ."

Her words stung Gabe a little, although at the same time he read the invitation in them. "Naomi," the other woman broke in, "if he wants to ride with us . . ."

Naomi smiled. "Yes . . . if he wants to."

Once again, an oblique invitation. Gabe nodded, pulled his horse up alongside the moving buggy. The girl drove at a steady pace, eyes on the rough track ahead. Her dress was slipping again, showing the top half of a breast. Either she spent time naked in the sun, or her skin was naturally an olive color. The older woman noticed the dress and jerked it back into place.

Gabe smiled. Up until now he'd been avoiding the local people as much as they'd been avoiding him. Now, quite by chance, he'd met people that interested him. He'd already noticed that the girl was the only one of the three who did not speak with an accent. True, the man and woman's accent was not particularly strong, nor was it unpleasant, but it was noticeable. He couldn't quite place it, although he suspected that the accent might identify them as being from Germany. Or perhaps east of Germany, from one of those middle European countries that his study of history told him changed in size and territory quite often, usually violently. Wherever they were from, he felt comfortable with them; they seemed solid, honest.

After half an hour's riding, they reached a small collection of buildings. None of the buildings were large, nor did they reflect wealth, but there was an almost painful neatness about them. Gabe saw a fine little barn, and healthy animals in pens and corrals. The farmhouse itself sat on a slight rise, its neat sides surrounded by flowers and shrubbery.

While Gabe dismounted, then tethered his horse to a railing, Hans got out of the buggy with only a little aid from the women. He walked inside, with Naomi lightly holding his right arm. Gabe remained standing by his horse, watching. The older woman, finally tearing her eyes away from Hans, noticed him. "Please," she said. "You must come inside. I will make some tea."

Her invitation appeared sincere, so Gabe followed her into the house. Inside, it was even cleaner than outside. The wooden floor shone from polishing. Beautifully crocheted doilies and antimacassars adorned rather worn and utilitarian furniture. Much of the furniture looked handmade, but was of excellent workmanship. Gabe had been inside quite a few Western homes, but this was not the usual grubby hovel. There were no signs of wealth; these people apparently had little to spare, but what they did have, they obviously treated with respect.

Hans sat on a kitchen chair, while Naomi poured water from a pitcher into an enamel basin. The older woman dipped a clean white cloth into the water and started wiping blood from the ragged wound on the side of the old man's head.

"Ow!" he grunted. "Eva . . . a little more care, please."

"Hans," the woman replied, "you'd complain even if someone was stuffing money in your pocket."

Gabe had three names now: Hans, Naomi, Eva. He walked over to a corner and leaned against a wall, arms folded over his chest, while he watched the two women patch up Hans. He'd thought of Hans as an old man before, but now saw that it was Hans's thick shock of white hair that had prompted that judgment. Yes, he had to be about sixty or sixty-five, but he had a strong-looking body and a relatively unlined face. The woman, Eva, who was most likely his wife, was a few years younger. Although her dark hair was heavily shot with gray, her face still had a calm, if somewhat careworn, beauty. As for Naomi, Gabe placed her age at twenty, perhaps just a little older. Studying the three of them, Gabe could see a resemblance, see something of Naomi in Eva's large dark eyes, see something of the girl in Hans's solid body. Yet, she seemed too young to be their daughter. And it was Naomi alone who had that something else in her eyes, that alert, aware strength.

Gabe watched while Naomi went over to a cupboard and took out a bottle of clear liquid. "Naomi," Hans protested, "that's for special occasions, just for drinking."

The girl shook her head. "Not this time, Grampa." That was it, then, she was their granddaughter. Lovely to look at. Gabe watched her heavy dark hair swing from side to side; she wore it tied behind her head. He saw the way points of light reflected from its glossy thickness. "This *is* a special occasion," she insisted. "Lean over a little."

Grumbling, Hans did as she requested. The girl poured some of the liquid into a small glass. Gabe could smell the sharp odor of alcohol. He watched as Naomi poured the alcohol directly into the wound. "Yow!" Hans yelped, grimacing. "That stings!"

"Good," Eva said sternly. "If it hurts, it must be good for you."

As Naomi turned to put the bottle back in the cupboard, she caught Gabe's eye, smiled. He permitted himself a small, answering smile. But he was annoyed. Mostly at Hans's behavior. Gabe had been brought up to despise pain, most of all, to despise those who showed that they felt pain. Among the Oglala, a man, even a boy, who cried out when hurt, was considered less than a woman. He remembered his earlier training. When he'd still been quite small, his father, to teach him courage, had placed burning seeds on his forearm. For a boy, the pain had been so great that Gabe still didn't know how he'd found the courage not to cry out. But he had found the strength—by then he'd already begun to learn courage—and as the lessons in courage continued, he also learned contempt for those without the same kind of stoicism with which he'd grown up.

Gabe was surprised then, when despite his earlier complaining, Hans sat poker-faced while Eva sewed up his wound with thick white thread and a big needle. Gabe noticed an exchange of very personal smiles between Eva and Hans, even as the needle was moving in and out of Hans's flesh, and it came to Gabe that there were other forms courage might take, less noticeable ones. Hans appeared to be so certain of his own courage that he could afford to show his pain when he chose to, and at other times, to ignore it.

Eva looked up from her work, saw Gabe watching. "Naomi," she said. "We are being bad hosts. Make our guest some tea."

The girl started a little, and Gabe became aware that she'd been watching him. Quite intently. Now she moved quickly to the sink, filled a pot with water, and placed it on the cookstove. Eva watched her with some exasperation. "It will not heat if you do not light the fire."

Naomi flushed. With her dark skin, it was an impressive change of coloration, more of depth of shade than an actual color change. For the first time, Gabe saw the girl a little flustered, and he sensed that he was the cause. The thought did not displease him.

The girl poked some shavings and kindling into the stove's firebox, touched a match to it, and soon had a small blaze going. She looked around for wood, saw none, and started for the door. When she had gone, Eva smiled at Gabe and said, "She likes you."

Now Gabe found himself flushing, but fought it down. He glanced at Hans, who was not smiling, but was looking at him speculatively. Judging him? Perhaps. "We owe you a lot," Hans said, almost defensively, as if to really say, "But hands off my beloved granddaughter."

"You owe me nothing," Gabe replied. "Only what one person normally owes another."

Hans seemed not to hear. "That trouble out there . . . it should not have happened," he said, almost musingly. "Those four men. . . . In the Old Country, I could understand such a thing, the hirelings of the local landowner. . . . But here? In this free land?"

"You knew those men?" Gabe asked.

Hans shrugged. "By sight only. We know of them as men who work for the railroad. Who work for Jethro Davis. He owns the railroad."

Gabe said nothing, merely nodded politely. He did not see the connection. Hans, aware of this, looked up at Eva. "Are you finished with torturing me, woman?" he asked. She had apparently set her last stitch and was using a pair of large scissors to cut off the thread close to the wound. When she said nothing, Hans got to his feet, a little shakily, and moved toward the bottle Naomi had used to sterilize his wound. "As Naomi said," he murmured, "this is a special occasion."

He looked almost defiantly at Eva as he poured a little of that clear liquid into a glass. He looked over at Gabe, while holding up the bottle. "A little for you, too?"

"No thank you," Gabe replied politely. He had a loathing for alcohol, never drank it. He'd seen what alcohol had done to his people, how it had turned brave, honorable warriors into drunken animals, who would sell their wives and daughters for another drink.

Hans seemed almost relieved. Apparently this bottle was a rare treasure for him. Gabe watched him sip from his glass, saw the look of pleasure on his face.

By now, Naomi had come back into the house, with an armful of wood. She began to poke smaller pieces into the stove. Hans took another sip. "It's the railroad," he finally said, sitting back down on his chair, glass still in hand. "They want our land."

"Not our land, Hans," Eva cut in. "In the eyes of the law, it's still their land."

Hans's face reddened. "Not in the eyes of true justice. Not in the eyes of God."

Naomi looked up from the stove. "God seems to have very little time for us lately," she said.

"Naomi! Don't talk that way," Eva remonstrated, but with very little heat.

"Ach," Hans said sadly. "Perhaps she is a little right. To think that this country, the land of liberty, would . . ."

He took another sip, then turned to face Gabe. "The rails were built through here about eight years ago. At the time, this was a wilderness, no one around for hundreds of miles, just a few Indians. Of course, a railroad going from nowhere to nowhere does not prosper. It needs people, to raise crops, to ship those crops, to have supplies shipped to them. People to ride the coaches. All the railroad had were those iron rails. And land. Lots of land. Given to them by the government, to encourage them to build. You are familiar with how that works?"

Gabe nodded. It was risky, building railroads into uninhabited land. Risky and expensive. The only incentive the federal government had to encourage such risk was land. Millions of square miles of government-owned land. Politicians tended to be lavish with that land, bestowing huge tracts on railroad companies. Supposedly empty land. Gabe had been annoyed when Hans had said the land had been empty . . . except for a few Indians. To the Indians, it had not seemed empty at all. It had been full of life, of plants, animals, rivers. Of the graves of their ancestors.

"Well," Hans continued, "the railroad offered land to any takers. Offered it for sale, no money down, the buyers to pay for it later, in a few years, when they had put in crops, buildings, when they had an income. A wonderful idea. Good, cheap land for farmers, and customers for the railroad."

Eva snorted derisively. "Not as wonderful as the idea they have now. Which is simple theft."

Hans nodded sadly, took another sip. "They quoted us a low price when we agreed to take this land. We were so happy to have it. Wonderful land, and so much of it. Much more than people of our class could ever hope to have in the Old Country. And how we worked to improve it, how we built, plowed, cultivated. Not just us, but others, too, tricked by those lying railroad men, those men of business, those thieves."

"Hans, you're rambling," Eva said. "You shouldn't drink that stuff."

Hans looked at her sternly, took another sip. Gabe noticed Naomi smiling affectionately as she stole a glance at the two older people. Apparently they were in the midst of an old, rather unimportant argument concerning Hans's precious bottle.

Hans turned back to face Gabe. "When the time was up, when it was time for us to pay for our land with the money we had saved, those railroad thieves told us that we had not really understood, that the price for the land would be higher. Much higher. More than any of us could pay. And if we did not pay, the land would go back to the railroad. Land we had sweated for, land we had made rich and valuable with our work. They had originally given us worthless wilderness, and now they would take back from us not only the land, but all our labor, too. And we would be left with nothing. Just wasted years. Simply to satisfy the greed of men already rich."

Another sip. Hans sat in his chair, morosely staring at the polished floorboards. Gabe looked away. He did not know what to say. To him, it was an old story. The story of the White Man's greed, his insatiable desire to have more and more, as if a man could eat more than a certain amount, as if he needed to walk over vast tracts of land he called his *own*. Wear more clothes, wield more power. The same old story. Greed, acquisition, the White Man's gods.

"And those four men?" Gabe asked. "The ones who attacked you?"

"Sent by Davis," Hans said bitterly. "To encourage us to leave. We have refused to give up our land. Only a few have decided to leave. And none have paid those higher prices. How could a man give in to . . ."

"Yes," Eva murmured. "A man must have his pride, mustn't he? Even if it gets his granddaughter . . . molested."

Hans looked angrily at his wife. "Why do you say that, Eva? You know that you do not want to leave, either."

She slowly nodded her head. "No, I do not. But I am afraid that our stubbornness will cost us a great deal. They have so much power, those railroad men."

Hans apparently had no answer to that. He sat silently, sipping the last of his drink. Gabe didn't know what to say. He felt sympathy for these people, even if they might have changed this land in a way he didn't like. They were honorable people. They clearly loved their land. On the way to the farmhouse, he'd seen how this particular farm took up most of a small valley, and how well the land had been cared for. He felt a slow anger building inside himself against greedy men who could so carelessly blight the lives of others, simply for money and power, two very useless things, unless a person also had honor, a sense of rightness.

Naomi broke the mood. "Do you like milk in your tea?" she asked.

Gabe turned toward her, bemused. He didn't even know if he liked tea; he'd drunk it so seldom. The girl was pouring from a pot into four delicate cups. The thought of milk in that dark liquid sickened him a little. "No," he replied. "Just tea."

She picked up a cup, brought it to him. He realized, as she handed him the cup, that she was standing much closer to him than necessary. He could actually feel the heat of her body. She looked up at him. At a distance, her eyes had been impressive. Close up, they were awesome, looking straight into his, with a frankness—and with something else hard to describe—that reached right inside his mind, his body. Gabe was no stranger to women, but this girl confused him. What was she offering? Or was she offering anything at all?

He made a decision, then, that he would stay in this valley for a while and find out.

CHAPTER THREE

Gabe was invited to stay for dinner. Once he'd accepted—he was very hungry—Eva and Naomi immediately set to work in the kitchen, after Naomi had changed out of her torn dress, a distinct disappointment to Gabe. On Hans's invitation, Gabe put his horse in the barn, unsaddling the animal, and rubbing him down. Before going back to the house, he took off his duster. Now, in addition to the pistol that rested, butt forward, on his right hip, another pistol came into view, a mate to the first, this one housed in a shoulder holster, hanging butt down, beneath his right armpit. Nor were the two pistols and the rifles the totality of his armament. The bone handle of a large knife protruded from a sheath that had been sewn to the side of the shoulder holster.

Gabe quickly pulled off the shoulder harness and stuffed it, pistol, knife, and all, into his saddlebags. He laid the saddlebags in a corner, then covered them with his duster. He hesitated a moment before leaving the barn, then picked up both rifles and took them with him to the house. Eva looked a little shocked when he brought the rifles inside, but Hans nodded in agreement. He had already taken down an old shotgun, which had been hanging over the fireplace, and loaded it.

The food was good, and there was lots of it. Gabe had not sat down at a table like this, with a family, for some time. At first he felt a little self-conscious, as if he had intruded someplace where he did not belong, but the others, Eva especially, seemed determined to make him feel at home. After some small talk, in which it became clear that Gabe did not want to talk about himself, the conversation turned toward the problem with the railroad, including accounts of people who'd been scared off their land, and of others who were resisting and in trouble. Gabe soon had a picture of a small group of thugs terrorizing the entire local population. "And the law?" Gabe asked. "What does the law do about all this?"

Hans snorted. "The law? Our local sheriff belongs to Jethro Davis, heart and soul. Well, wallet, mostly. Turns his eyes the other way."

"Too bad you can't get a new sheriff."

"Well, we could," Eva broke in. "Elections are coming up soon."

Hans shook his head. "It would be hard to find someone willing to run against Davis's tame sheriff. Too dangerous."

"Tom!" Naomi said vehemently. "Tom Olafson would make a good sheriff. And I think he has the guts to run."

"Naomi," Eva said sternly. "Watch your language."

Naomi flushed. "Oh . . . the heck with my language. If we could just talk Tom into running, there's enough of us to elect him. Then we'd have the law on our side."

Hans shook his head again. "You saw those men today." He turned toward Gabe. "There are more than the four you saw, and they have more guns between them than all the rest of us put together. They're professional killers. If Tom declared for sheriff, they'd . . . what's the word they use here? They'd bushwhack him."

"Not if they were kept very busy," Gabe murmured, looking off into space.

"What?" Hans asked.

Gabe looked down at his plate. "Nothing. I was just . . . thinking."

He was aware of a look of renewed interest directed his way by Naomi. It was a look of both excitement and curiosity. "But somebody could . . ." she started to say, then stopped when Hans shot her a warning glance. Perhaps Hans might have followed the subject himself, less impulsively than the girl, but he was obviously beginning to tire; his head seemed to be hurting him. Gabe watched Hans bring his hand to his forehead.

"A good meal, Eva," Hans said. "As it always is. And, as always, your dinner has made me very sleepy."

He looked apologetically at Gabe. "I hope you will excuse me, I can think only of bed."

Gabe was a little surprised that a man who'd been beaten as badly as Hans had managed to stay on his feet this long. He was obviously tougher than Gabe had first believed. Gabe stood up, looked out the door. In another half hour it would be dark. "It's time I saddled my horse . . . rode on. . . ."

Eva seemed genuinely shocked. "You will do no such thing! I'm afraid there's not much room in the house, but in the barn you will be out of the weather."

Gabe did not bother to tell Eva that sleeping outdoors was what he preferred. However, the meal had been a heavy one, and the thought of saddling his horse and looking for a place to set up camp for the night was not attractive. Besides, there was still Naomi, those eyes, the way they had been appraising him all during supper. He would like to see if her eyes sent him the same message in the morning. In addition, perhaps the four men he'd run off might come back for revenge. Hans, with his old shotgun, would be no match for them.

Before the dishes were even cleared away, Naomi went to fetch a lantern. The house was indeed small: kitchen, living room, a large bedroom for Hans and Eva, and a much smaller room, off at the far end of the living room, which was Naomi's. While Eva helped Hans, who was now acting slightly dizzy, toward their bedroom, Naomi picked up a lantern, then led Gabe outside. It was dusk, and quite dark inside the barn; the lantern was a necessity. The barn, while small, was as neat and clean inside as it was outside. Naomi guided Gabe toward a stack of hay at the rear of the barn, inside a stall. "It's not much of a bed," she said. "But it's a lot better than the hard ground."

He didn't argue with her; indeed, the hay was new and clean. Naomi was carrying a blanket. After Gabe had leaned his rifles against the side of the stall, he and Naomi flattened out the mound of hay, then spread the blanket out over it. They straightened, at opposite ends of the blanket, then stood awkwardly for a moment, looking everywhere but at each other, aware that they were standing above his bed. Finally, as if to break the tension, Naomi pointed toward the rifles. "Do you take them everywhere with you?" she asked, half in amusement, half seriously.

"Everywhere."

She nodded. "Even to bed. I pity your wife. If you have one." She looked straight into his eyes. "Do you?" she asked. "Have a wife?"

He met her gaze squarely. "I once had a wife," he replied, his voice flat.

"Oh?"

"She was . . . killed."

There must have been something in his eyes, some expression that reflected the way he had felt that day, the day he saw his wife die. Naomi recoiled, moved back a step. "I . . . I'm sorry."

He said nothing. She turned to go, then turned back, studying him. "I'm glad that you're here, that you helped us." Then she turned again and walked away. Gabe watched her all the way out of the barn, watched until she had disappeared into the gathering darkness outside.

He remained standing for a moment, then picked up his bedroll and unrolled it on top of the blanket he and Naomi had laid down on the straw. He unbuckled his gun belt, placed it next to his bed, along with the rifles. It was a warm night, so he took off his moccasins, trousers, shirt, and underwear, then slipped into the bedroll, naked.

Soogan. That's what the White Man called a bedroll. Along with other names, Gabe remembered, like fart sack. Appropriate to the bean-and-bacon-eating cowhand. Gabe had made his own bedroll out of some army blankets and wool fleece. When he'd lived with the People, he'd slept beneath a massive buffalo robe, warm and snug inside that mound of black fleece, but he found the soogan lighter, more transportable. He had no lodge to return to now, with its warm fire and waiting buffalo robes. No wife nor mother to keep a lodge. . . .

Yellow Buckskin Girl. His Oglala wife. Naomi's question had brought back her memory. He suddenly became aware of something about Naomi that had been bothering him . . . her eyes were a little like Yellow Buckskin Girl's eyes. There were other similarities that now became apparent to him. True, Yellow Buckskin Girl's skin color had been a little darker than the white girl's, and her hair straighter and blacker. She had been all Lakota, all Oglala. A Sioux, as the White Men said. Maybe it was because of Yellow Buckskin Girl that Gabe had so often been attracted to dark-eyed, dark-haired women. Moving restlessly within his bedroll, he remembered his Oglala wife's face, the silky texture of her skin, the smell of her body, sweet and musky at the same time. He remembered the way she cried out when they made love. . . .

With these images came another image, a much uglier image. Of a bullet hitting her in the forehead, knocking her backward. Of her falling, dead, never to laugh again, cry, make love, never to do any of the things that separate the living from the dead. And he thought of his mother, dying by his wife's side, run through by Price's saber. The horror of it. . . .

Gabe tore his mind away from those terrible images. Better not to remember, better to live on with a mind wiped clean of the past . . . if that could be called living. Damn, why had Naomi asked him if he had a wife?

He concentrated on what was currently around him, the sweet smell of the hay, the distant, mournful hooting of a hunting owl, followed by the thin shriek of some small animal dying. There, that was better. Dying was a part of the world. The People had always known that, known they would not live forever. Still, the pain of it all. . . .

Gabe fell asleep in mid-thought, and did not dream, his memories eclipsed by the night. He had been asleep for over an hour when the barn door slowly opened. A figure stood in the doorway, waiting, then finally stepped into the dimness of the barn and began moving toward where Gabe was sleeping. The barn door hinges, like most other hinges on this neat little farm, had been well oiled, so there had been little noise when the door opened. And the footsteps moving toward Gabe's bed-roll were muffled by the softness of the straw which partially covered the floor. Nevertheless, Gabe was almost instantly aware of the intrusion; he would not have lived this long if he were not constantly alert to every movement around him, even when asleep.

He came out of sleep instantly, any grogginess held at bay as he reached for the butt of the pistol next to his bedroll. It was not completely dark in the barn, a shaft of moonlight shone in through an opening high in one wall, illuminated the figure approaching. A figure dressed in white.

Gabe pulled back the hammer of his pistol. The harsh double click stopped the figure in its tracks. "Oh!" a voice said, startled.

It was the girl. Naomi. Wearing a nightgown. Gabe eased the hammer down, lowered the pistol's muzzle. "Why are you . . .? Is there trouble at the house?" he asked.

"I . . . no," she replied, somewhat haltingly, as if not quite sure of herself. "I . . . wanted to talk to you some more, I . . ."

Her voice died away. She remained standing for a moment, silent, then sank down onto her knees next to Gabe's bedroll. In the moonlight, her eyes were huge dark pools, unreadable, but he was able to sense the tension in her body. And pretty sure about what was causing it. Desire.

She was quite close. He reached up, gently stroked her hair, which was hanging loose and long over her shoulders. She shivered at his touch. "I," she said haltingly. "You know, I really shouldn't be . . ."

He was propped up on one elbow. Her eyes moved over his naked chest, then back up to his face. He could see a little of the expression in her eyes now; she looked like a startled doe. Apprehensive, perhaps afraid that he was going to reject her. Instead, he moved over in the bedroll, folded the top part back to make room. She immediately slid into the bedroll, uttering a grateful little sigh. There was not much room; they were, by necessity, very close together. He felt the warmth of her body against his own, radiating through the thin cotton nightgown.

Yet, despite the heat of her skin, she still seemed tense, nervous. "You see," she said, "it's just that it's so . . . isolated out here."

Then the words came in a rush. "I could live my entire life out, day after day, year after year, with nothing to . . . nothing of my very own, nothing to make me feel *alive*. And," she added, in a voice a little less rushed, a little deeper, "since the first time I saw you, you made me think about being alive. You made me think about . . . my body."

Gabe kissed her. She seemed a little surprised at first, as if she were not already in bed with him. Her lips were warm and soft, at first closed, then they parted, and her mouth moved on his. All hesitation seemed to leave the girl. When Gabe started pulling her nightgown up over her head, she cooperated, wriggling inside the bedroll to make it easier.

Now she was naked; they were skin to skin. Shuddering, she pressed harder against him, her mouth seeking his again.

The confined space of the bedroll was proving an impediment. Without either needing to say anything, they slid out of the bedroll, rolled onto the blanket. The hay was soft beneath them, just a little of it prickling through the blanket.

Naomi looked at Gabe. "I'm . . . not a virgin," she said, her voice slightly tense.

"Neither am I," he replied, smiling.

She laughed then, and after that it was easy, their bodies came together naturally.

When it was over, they lay joined together for another minute or two, neither of them thinking much about the passage of time. Finally, Gabe rolled free, lying on his back next to the girl. He looked over at her, saw the way her dark hair, made darker by the night, spread out over the blanket, saw how her breasts were still rising and falling from the force of her breathing. As he'd noticed earlier in the day—each time her torn dress had fallen open—they were not particularly large breasts, but they were perfectly formed, and a little swollen now after their lovemaking. Gabe let his eyes travel down the rest of the girl's body. It was a full body, not fat, but generous through the hips. A woman's body, not a girl's. She might widen considerably as she got older, but at the moment he considered her perfect.

Slowly, they began to talk, to learn about one another. She told him that she was twenty-two years old, and that the family name was Karstedt. Hans and Eva were her grandparents. Her father, their son, along with his wife, had died in a smallpox epidemic when Naomi was a little girl. She had lived with them ever since. To her, they were her parents. "They're wonderful people," she said. "They left a lot behind them in Europe. They were cultured people; Hans especially is very well educated. They had a good position in life. But . . . some very bad things must have happened. They had to leave. Leave everything of their life behind. They will not talk about it, but I think it must have been very bad. I think there was a lot of killing."

Without a doubt, Gabe thought. Perhaps that was what had initially drawn him to Hans and Eva, the sense that they too had seen their people destroyed. And survived to live an alien life among alien people.

"I think Hans taught me too many things," the girl continued. "Taught me to look at the world in a way that's not good for a farm girl. To think about the big world out there, about art, music, adventure. That's why, when there's a chance to . . . feel something, to have . . . experiences, that I . . . well, I sometimes take these chances."

Then she hastily added, reinforcing Gabe's opinion that she wasn't quite the woman of the world she might think herself, "But . . . only once in a while!"

Now that Naomi had told a little about herself, she gave her fascination over Gabe a free rein. "I noticed your finger at dinner," she said. "What happened to it?"

Gabe held up his right hand. The index finger had been broken at the first joint, which pointed away from the other fingers at a ninety-degree angle. "I broke it hitting a man on the jaw," he said laconically. He said it that way to tease her, because he knew he was going to tell her many things about himself, things he normally did not tell others. Why? Perhaps because he felt a closeness to her, perhaps because he had been alone much too long.

She sensed that he was teasing her. She poked him in the ribs. "Uh-uh. You're not going to get off that easy. I want to know about you. For instance, how come you look so . . . different? Kind of like an Indian."

"Because I am. An Oglala Sioux."

She looked skeptically at his long, sandy-colored hair, those pale gray eyes, and poked him again. So he told her. How his mother and father, both white, had entered the Black Hills, along with a small group of other white people, looking for gold. And how a local band of Oglalas, the Bad Faces, to whom the Black Hills was sacred ground, had attacked the intruders, killing all of them with the exception of Gabe's mother, Amelia. How Amelia's courage had caused one of the Bad Faces to spare her life, and take her for his woman. And how Amelia had already been pregnant with Gabe at the time of the attack. "She told me that she'd probably only been pregnant a few minutes before the attack started," Gabe told Naomi. "She and my father had . . . woken up a little earlier. So I was born among the Oglala. It was wild land, then, up there in what they now call the Dakotas. She knew there was no way out, that I would grow up among the People. So she helped me become a good Oglala. Except she taught me to speak and read and write English. Until I was older, I never knew I was anything other than a Lakota. Of course, a Lakota with funny-looking hair and eyes. But my mother made that all right, she told me that she and I had caught part of the sun's light. That was enough for me."

"But," Naomi said, "you obviously went back to your own people, eventually."

"No!" he said more sharply than he intended. "I left my people and went to live among strangers. Because my people were no more, they had been destroyed by greed and hatred. They were destroyed so that the White Man could steal their land."

He was immediately sorry he'd spoken so sharply; he could sense Naomi's discomfort. So he said, more softly, "My mother saw the White Men start to come into our country. Better than any of us, she realized their strength. So, since she didn't want me killed fighting the soldiers, she sent me to an army post to live with the whites. Tricked me into going there," he added, surprised that after all these years, he still felt bitterness. "The soldiers treated me like a slave. Locked me in jail when I defended myself against one of their officers. But I finally escaped, finally found the People again."

They both fell silent. Naomi moved closer against him, as if physical closeness would close the gaps in their two very different lives. She began to trace her fingers over his flesh, over his chest. It helped him to relax. Then her fingertips found the long, thin scars that crisscrossed his arms and chest, scars difficult to see in the moonlight, but obvious to her touch. "How did you get these?" she asked.

"I made them myself."

He could sense that was not going to be enough of an answer. "It is an Oglala custom," he said. "When you suffer a great loss. That day, when my wife was killed, my mother too, I cut myself with my knife, to show my grief. Cut my hair off."

"Oh! I . . . I shouldn't have asked. . . ."

He continued anyway. "Not long after I'd returned from the fort, the soldiers attacked. Attacked at dawn. Attacked a sleeping camp of peaceful people. Surprised people. The soldiers killed and killed. Men, women, children. My wife was shot in the stomach first, then in the head. The same soldier killed my mother with a saber. I was not able to stop it."

Naomi shivered, then moved even closer, as if to shelter herself from the horror of what he had said, by reassuring herself with the reality of his body. They lay together for a while, until Naomi finally stirred. "I better go back to the house. Sometimes Eva gets up during the night. She . . . would be worried."

Gabe watched the girl put on her nightgown. Her movements were very graceful, and he could sense her happiness over what had happened between them. Dressed, she knelt by him. She bent down to kiss him, and when she straightened again, she said, "I know that this is only for a little while. I know that you'll go away again some day. It's your nature. I can tell. But it's worth it to me, to have what it is of you that I'll have. For this moment, I'm very happy."

She stood, and without another word, walked away. In the moonlight she seemed to float across the floor, her long hair hanging down black against the white of her nightgown. A moment later she was out the door, leaving Gabe wondering if he might have dreamed the whole thing. Only the sweet scent of her, clinging to his skin, completely convinced him.

CHAPTER FOUR

Gabe woke just as the first light of dawn began filtering into the barn. He lay on his back, arms behind his head, looking up at the wooden roof beams. He felt good, relaxed. It was a fine thing for a man to make love to a woman. No doubt fine for the woman, too, if the way Naomi had reacted was any guide. For a few minutes he relived mental images of Naomi's naked body, of her dark hair and eyes, of her passion.

He also remembered how much he had told her about himself. Well, he had no regrets about that; it had been a two-way street. She'd helped remind him that he had a past that he valued.

Of course, he hadn't told her everything. He held up his right hand. She'd been intrigued by the broken finger, eager for stories of adventure. She hadn't noticed the puckered scar in the center of the palm; he hadn't bothered to point it out, nor had he mentioned that the scar had been made by a pitchfork in the hands of the same man on whose jaw he'd broken his finger a few minutes later. Captain Stanley Price, a bully and a coward. Price, bested twice by a boy, burning with a terrible desire for revenge. A revenge he'd realized later, because it was Price who'd killed Gabe's mother and Yellow Buckskin Girl, his wife. After Gabe had tracked him down, Price had paid terribly, but it had not brought either woman back to life. However, Gabe had learned a lesson that would stay with him forever . . . never leave an enemy alive. His failure to kill Price when he'd had the chance had cost the lives of the two people Gabe loved the most.

Enough. Gabe let his right hand drift over to the Sharps carbine that lay next to his Winchester. A gift from someone else he'd come to love. Jim Bridger, the scout. A man he'd hated at first, because it was Bridger who'd kidnapped him from his lodge, who'd taken him to the fort . . . at the request of Gabe's own mother. It had taken Gabe a long time to forgive his mother, to recognize the wisdom and selflessness of her choice.

It had taken less time to forgive Bridger. Gabe remembered how grateful he'd felt when Bridger had stepped into the barn, Sharps in hand, just in time to keep Gabe from being shot in the back by Price's fellow officers. The sound of the carbine's heavy hammer being cocked had frozen the officers in place. Then Gabe had beaten Price unconscious, breaking the trigger finger of his wounded hand in the process.

But, he'd left Price alive. He angrily discarded the thought. What was past was past; he could not let his mind dwell on old mistakes. Later, after he'd killed Price, he'd atoned to some extent by fighting at the side of the People against the army. Gabe smiled as he thought about Crazy Horse, his friend, his comrade in arms. Crazy Horse, the man of visions. Gabe stopped smiling. Crazy Horse was dead now, murdered by soldiers the moment he lay down his arms.

No, better to forget that, too. Forget lost causes. Better to think about Naomi. She was different than most of the white women he'd met, more open, less constrained by the rigid social rules that tended to turn them into frigid blocks of ice. Gabe wondered if he would have another chance to make love to the girl. Probably . . . when she'd left last night, her eyes had been full of unspoken promises.

Of course, she was probably using him, well, perhaps just a little, using her beauty, her body, to enlist his aid against her family's enemy, the railroad. She might not even be aware of it, but he sensed the possibility. Not that it mattered to him. She was only doing what women did by nature. Society, and a lack of physical strength, kept them from acting in a more direct manner.

No, it didn't matter, because he'd already decided to help these people, this Karstedt family, against the men who were brutalizing them, brutalizing most of the people of the region. This was what Gabe had been trained to do, protect the weak from the strong. To be a warrior. To fight against evil, and what could be more evil than the White Man's everlasting greed, that sickness of the soul that victimized the powerless, that drove those already strong and rich to accumulate more and more and more.

Yes, he would fight. That would be good; he had been following an aimless, lonely road far too long. He would come alive again as a warrior. Perhaps his meeting of the Karstedt's had been a gift from *Wakan-tanka,* that mysterious power the White Man called the Great Spirit. Yes, perhaps this chance to fight again was a gift from his old life.

Then there was the girl, Naomi, in herself enough to make a man feel grateful to be alive. To remind a man there were still things worth fighting for. Of course, he might get killed. Gabe shrugged. While he did not court death, neither did he fear it. After all, wasn't death an inescapable part of life? He had grown up hearing that old Lakota saying, "Only the rocks live forever," repeated again and again. No, death was not that important. Most important was to live with dignity. Gabe nodded. It was not the length of a man's life that counted, but the manner in which he lived it.

Gabe slipped out of his bedroll, but before dressing he went over to a horse trough and quickly washed his lower body. Fighting lay ahead, and a man who was foolish enough to go into a fight after having made love to a woman without washing himself first was a man asking for death. Or so the People had taught him. And that was enough for Gabe, for, despite the many books he had read, despite his studies of the White Man's wisdom, he had found nothing in those books or the White Man's beliefs that spoke to him more directly than Lakota ways. The ways that connected a man to the marvelous, mysterious world around him, a world free of clumsy abstractions, free of an endless stream of meaningless words. Gabe smiled. The day was starting well.

When Gabe walked into the house, everyone was already up, even Hans, with his head bound up in a bandage. "Behold the mummy," Hans said as Gabe came inside.

Gabe smiled, nodded, then glanced quickly at Naomi. She was putting plates on the table. She looked up to meet his gaze, smiled slightly, then concentrated again on her work. Gabe glanced quickly at Eva, who was cooking. She merely smiled, then turned to stir a pot.

Breakfast was big, made up of oatmeal, milk, bread, coffee, sausages, and eggs. Gabe ate lightly; he did not like to eat much in the morning. He savored the coffee; that was something the White Man had that he appreciated.

"Those men," Gabe said abruptly. "The ones who attacked you. Where do they stay?"

Hans looked up sharply. "Why do you ask?"

Gabe calmly returned Hans's gaze. "Not so that I can avoid them."

Hans flushed. "I never thought that. But I'm a little concerned about you getting tangled up in our troubles."

"I read somewhere in a book," Gabe replied, "that one man's trouble concerns all men."

Particularly when a woman like Naomi comes to you in the night, he added silently. He glanced over at the girl, to find her already looking at him. She smiled again. Something warm and sensual flashed in her eyes. Hans did not miss it, nor did Eva. Hans and Eva looked at one another, then Eva turned a questioning gaze on Naomi, who blushed and looked away.

Hans stiffened a little. Gabe waited for the usual angry outburst, sad that he had already used up his welcome in this house. How strange the White Man was, with his fanaticism about virginity.

But Hans quickly recovered. "There's a town about ten miles further west. Most of the time, Davis's hired killers hang around the biggest saloon, drinking, gambling . . . when they're not out terrorizing people. They stay at a hotel. Davis pays for their rooms."

"Does Davis stay there, too?"

"No. He has a big place further north. Bigger town, the county seat. That's where the sheriff is, too."

"So, the sheriff isn't usually around to back up Davis's men?"

"No. . . . Why? Are you thinking of going there?"

Gabe smiled. "I need supplies."

Hans was silent a moment. "They'll recognize you. There'll be trouble. You can't go there by yourself."

Now Naomi cut in; she was no longer smiling. "There are always several of them there," she said vehemently. "You could get . . . killed."

"Perhaps," he replied. "Perhaps not. I promise you, I won't be stupid."

Everyone had lost interest in breakfast. Naomi's earlier happiness had changed to worry. Eva kept looking from her to Gabe. Hans looked embarrassed. "It's not a good feeling for a man . . . to have other men do his fighting for him," he said.

"Why not?" Gabe asked. "This railroad owner, Davis—doesn't he?"

Hans nodded wryly, but said nothing. Gabe got up from the table. "I'll ride in, just look around."

Hans shook his head. "It isn't going to be that easy," he repeated morosely.

When Gabe started out the door, Naomi followed him. "Naomi," Hans called after her, but Eva stepped close, put her hand on her husband's arm. "Let her go," she said in a soft voice. "Can't you see that she's a woman now?"

Gabe and Naomi walked out to the barn. Naomi stood to one side, hands clasped in front of her, head down, while Gabe packed his gear. Clearly, she was dejected. She had only wanted him to stay near, in case the men came back. But now . . . to go where they lived . . .

Her dejection turned to interest when Gabe took a black leather coat out of his saddlebags and put it on. It was quite long and hung down almost to the ground. But what interested her most was the design painted across the back of the coat, high up, a brightly colored and stylized figure of a huge bird, with its wings spread out over Gabe's shoulders. "What's that?" she asked.

Gabe hesitated. What could he say? That it was his War Coat? "Just a coat," he replied.

"No. I mean the picture on the back."

He reached back, touched the bright pigments. "*Wakinyan.* The Winged One. What the White Man calls the Thunder-bird."

"And you made the coat, painted it?"

"Yes and no," he replied. He told her how just before the army attacked the village, his mother had made a new lodge cover, out of buffalo hides. He didn't know why he told Naomi, perhaps it was because she had shared so much of herself the night before. "When my mother was making the lodge cover," he said, "I'd just finished a vision quest. *Wakinyan* was part of my vision, so she painted it onto the leather. She may have grown up a white woman, but she was Lakota now, and very proud I'd had such a powerful vision. Then later, after the attack, after my mother was . . . dead, the army burned the lodges, burned them along with the winter's food supply, so that the People would starve to death."

"They did that? The army?" Naomi burst out, clearly shocked. No doubt she'd been brought up on stories that portrayed the army as the settler's protector . . . which it was, at great cost to the Indians.

"Yes, they did just that," he said flatly. "And a lot more. But when those of us who survived came back to the village, I saw that part of my mother's lodge had not completely burned. The part with the painting of *Wakinyan.* I took that as a sign, because part of my vision was that *Wakinyan* would be my pro-tector. So I cut out the unburned part and made this coat."

She looked at him silently for a moment. He knew what she must be thinking: how could a white man believe pagan nonsense about the figure of a stylized bird, a pagan idol, pro-tecting a man? But she surprised him. "I hope this *Wakinyan* does a good job of protecting you, Gabe. Please don't get killed."

He smiled, put his arms around her, kissed her. She did not respond immediately, but then her lips parted and she kissed him passionately. He stepped back, looked down into her face. "I won't. If I did, I wouldn't be able to come back here, and . . . have another night with you. Like last night."

Naomi flushed furiously. "You be careful, then. I . . . I'll be waiting."

She watched while he saddled his horse, strapped the saddlebags and bedroll in place, then slid both rifles into their saddle scabbards. They walked side by side as he led his horse out of the barn. Hans and Eva stood on the porch, watching, as he mounted. They waved. He waved back, looked down at Naomi, smiled. "It's a promise, then? When I come back?"

She blushed again. "Yes," she said fiercely. "A promise."

He rode out of the farmyard, turned once to look back. Naomi had gone up onto the porch with her grandparents. Eva had an arm around the girl. Gabe nudged his horse into a canter, and when he looked back again, he could not see the farmhouse.

He shut his mind to anything except what lay ahead. A pleasurable sensation ran through his body, a sensation prompted by the expectation of danger. It was a familiar feeling; he'd had the same sensation many years before, again and again, each time he'd ridden out with an Oglala war or hunting party, when each man had been aware of the chance that death might strike at any moment. It was an awareness that always filled Gabe with a sense of his very aliveness, an awareness that heightened his senses, that infused the world around him with an immediacy, an imminence, an enhanced reality. Only a man's first love for a woman could come anywhere near equaling that feeling, and it was a poor second. And without that feeling, Gabe had long ago found that life held little interest for him.

Now, once again, the world was so incredibly alive. He listened to the soft chuckle of a nearby stream, the susurration of the breeze passing through the trees. He marveled at the way the sunlight struck each object in a slightly different, unique way. All around, the world was beautiful. He rode in beauty.

He was also very aware of the wings of *Wakinyan*, spreading over his shoulders, filling him with a sense of strength, protection. He had not mentioned to Naomi the bad parts of his vision, the foreknowledge that his mother would die, that he would be separated from the People. He'd been horrified, but then his horror had been deflected by the sound of giant wings beating above him. Looking up, he had seen *Wakinyan*, himself, the Winged One, hovering, just a few feet up. A moment later the god had settled over Gabe, folding his wings protectively about his shoulders, filling Gabe with a wonderful feeling of protection, of continuity. Even though Gabe would lose the People themselves, he would have this part of the old life with him always. The Thunderbird himself.

"Aaiiyah!" he called out softly. "This is a good day for fighting. A beautiful day to die."

CHAPTER FIVE

The town was an hour and a half's ride to the west. Gabe smelled it before he saw it, the sharp tang of many wood fires, plus the indefinable smell of a number of people living close together.

When he was still a couple of miles away, he headed toward high ground. Here, the land was quite hilly. The town itself was situated in a draw, where the river had cut a channel through an upthrust of rock. When Gabe had gained enough height, he saw a straggle of buildings below. He rode along an outcrop of rock that ran quite close to the town. It was a perfect vantage point. Thick bushes would conceal him; he could see without being seen.

Dismounting, Gabe tied his horse to a small tree. He rummaged in his saddlebags, came up with pair of binoculars, then walked to the edge of the outcrop, careful to make certain his movements were screened by the thickest of the bushes.

Lying on his belly, he looked down at the town. There was just one main street, dusty, rutted, with two very short streets running off at right angles. The buildings were of rickety frame construction. Although Hans had told him the town was fairly new, the unpainted wood of the buildings already looked weathered and old.

Packed into its narrow draw, the town would never grow very much. It had probably originally been situated here because of the stream, which provided water all year round. And also, because of the commanding position, blocking this small pass.

Gabe picked up his binoculars and began to study the town. Since he was only about four hundred yards away, the powerful lenses permitted him to read the signs on some of the buildings. He saw a hardware and feed store, a general store, a blacksmith's, and a straggle of other buildings whose function was difficult to guess. Further back, scattered here and there, were a few individual dwellings.

There was no mistaking the saloon. It was situated at the far end of the main street. The saloon and the hotel, looming up at opposite ends of the street, were the largest buildings in sight.

There was a certain amount of coming and going, mostly in and out of the hardware and general stores. The majority of the people on the street were men; few women were visible. Clearly, the town was less a place of habitation, and more of a supply center for the surrounding countryside.

Gabe watched a man leave the saloon, weaving, drunk already. Judging from his seedy appearance, he seemed to be a simple local drunk. The drunk wandered through the streets, finally disappearing into a dilapidated shack near the back edge of town.

Movement by the hotel. Gabe watched three men come out the hotel's front door. Two of them he instantly recognized as having been in the gang that had harassed the Karstedts.

The three men wandered into one of the smaller buildings. Half an hour later, they came back outside. Watching one of them wipe the back of his hand across his mouth, then break a splinter off a hitching rail and proceed to pick his teeth, Gabe realized that the building must house a restaurant.

The three men walked slowly along the street, in the direction of the saloon. Gabe noticed how the few ordinary-looking citizens they encountered gave them a wide berth. All three of the men were wearing pistols. One had a big bowie knife hanging in a sheath.

The three men went into the saloon. Figuring they might stay there a while, Gabe returned to his horse, reached into the saddlebags, and pulled out a tin container. Taking it back to the edge of the outcrop, he sat behind a bush, while keeping an eye on the town below, and opened the tin. It contained pemmican. Breaking a piece of wood off a small dead tree, Gabe shoveled a little of the pemmican into his mouth. He did not eat much; the pemmican was very rich. He'd made it himself, two weeks before, of dried beef, suet, crushed berries, and herbs.

When he was satisfied, he put the lid back on the tin . . . just as four more men came out of the hotel. They were men like the ones who had gone into the saloon. Picking up his glasses, he recognized two of them as the others who'd molested the Karstedts.

These men went through the same routine as the first three, stopping at the restaurant, then, half an hour later, going down the street to the saloon.

Seven of them so far. Gabe spent the next three hours watching the hotel. None of those going in or out seemed like gunmen. So maybe seven was all there were, unless there were others out terrorizing farmers.

Sometime after noon, all of the gunmen came out of the saloon and entered the restaurant. It must have been cramped inside, because Gabe saw them eject two men, who stood in the dusty street in front of the restaurant, looking angrily inside. But good sense made them walk away.

Half an hour later, four of the gunmen left the restaurant for the hotel, while three more went back to the saloon. For the rest of the day, there was a great deal of coming and going between the restaurant, the hotel, and the saloon. Gabe did his best to keep track of who was where. Finally, about half an hour before dark, by his count there were three in the hotel, two in the restaurant, and two in the saloon. And one of those in the saloon had been among the men who'd attacked Naomi and her grandparents.

Gabe moved quickly back to his horse. Putting away the binoculars, he took off his coat, then pulled his shoulder rig from the saddlebags and strapped it into place. He pulled the revolver out of the shoulder holster and checked it. It was a .44 caliber Colt revolver, as was the one riding on his right hip. He checked the loads, all six. Many men kept the chamber beneath

the hammer empty, to avoid accidental discharges, but Gabe
wanted the advantage of having one extra shot. After he'd
checked that each chamber was loaded, he eased the hammer
down, turning the cylinder with his fingers, so that the firing
pin sat between two chambers, instead of directly on top of a
primer.

He checked the other Colt, then the rifles. All were loaded,
all ready to cock and fire. He put his coat back on, concealing
the gun and knife in the shoulder rig. He mounted, then rode
down off the rear of the outcrop and turned toward the town.
He did not ride straight down the main street, but made a loop
around to the west, entering from the rear.

It was beginning to grow dark when he pulled up behind
the saloon. As he'd expected, there was a rear door. He dismounted, then tied his horse to a scrubby bush about twenty
yards from the saloon door.

He hesitated. He hated leaving his rifles, only a fool used
a pistol when a rifle was available, yet, inside the saloon, the
longer barrel of a rifle might get in the way. So he left both
the Sharps and the Winchester in their saddle scabbards. As
he walked away, he was a little worried about finding both
guns there when he returned, although he knew that his horse,
a mean-tempered animal, was not likely to let any strangers
approach too closely.

Gabe did not go into the saloon through the rear door.
Walking around the side of the building, he reached the town's
main thoroughfare. Looking around the corner, he studied the
street. It looked like two of the gunmen were still inside the
restaurant. How long they would stay there, he didn't know.

Gabe walked quickly to the saloon's front entrance. It was
a warm night; the door was open. Looking inside, he quickly
studied the interior. Just one large room. He could see the back
door clearly. No obstructions, and the door did not appear to
be locked.

A long bar ran down the left side of the room. There were
several rickety tables scattered here and there. Gabe saw two
of the gunmen sitting at one of the tables, near the rear of the
saloon, playing cards. Two whiskey bottles sat on the tabletop
between them, one empty, one half empty. There were two

other men inside the bar, each seated apart. They appeared to have no connection to the gunmen.

Gabe stepped into the saloon, stopped just inside the doorway, checking the walls to either side. Nobody there, no one to get behind him. One of the men seated alone looked up, gawked a little. Tall, powerfully built, with his sun-darkened skin and those pale gray eyes, wearing a big slouch hat and the long black buffalo-hide coat, Gabe made an imposing picture.

One of the gunmen looked up, glanced at Gabe, then his companion snarled at him to bet or fold. The gunman turned his attention back to his companion, snarled something back, and rang a dollar down on the tabletop. Amateurs, Gabe thought. Cheap bullies. A professional would have marked him the moment he walked in, and never let his attention waver until he was a known entity.

Gabe walked over to the bar. The bartender, a portly, bored-looking man about forty years old, wearing a phenomenally bushy, drooping moustache, came toward him, languidly polishing a chipped glass with a stained and torn rag. "What'll it be, stranger?" he asked, without much enthusiasm.

"Root beer," Gabe replied.

The bartender's mouth fell open. Gabe could make out the gleam of teeth through all that lip shrubbery. "What'd you say?" the bartender asked. "Root beer?"

"That's exactly what I said. If you don't have root beer, I'll take sarsaparilla."

The bartender looked as if he were about to say something clever. Until now, Gabe had been looking down or to the sides as he spoke. As a boy, he'd been taught that it was very impolite to stare someone straight in the eye. That was Oglala etiquette. He'd had a difficult time adapting to the White Man's eye to eye contact. But now he was beginning to grow a little annoyed. He hated alcohol, hated what it did to people, but he loved root beer. So he raised his head and looked the bartender straight in the eyes. The bartender, a smart rejoinder on his lips, found himself pinned by Gabe's gaze, staring into the coldest pair of eyes he'd ever seen. There was nothing at all there, just a flat hardness that scared the hell out of him. "Sure, mister," he said hurriedly. "One bottle o' root beer, coming up."

The scene at the bar had caused one of the men playing cards to look up. He was one of the men Gabe had faced down yesterday. For just a moment he stared at Gabe, confused, then he recognized him. "Hey, Hank!" he hissed to his companion. "That's the bastard we told you about. The one who threw down on us."

The other man looked up. Quite slowly, Gabe noticed. Both men had apparently been drinking most of the day. He'd already observed that most of their movements were slow. The second man, Hank, stared balefully at Gabe. "Well," he said to the other man, "I guess we know how to take care o' bushwhackers, don't we?"

Still, neither man stood up. Trying to get their sodden brains working, Gabe thought. Good, because he didn't want trouble before his root beer arrived. There it was now, thudding down onto the bar next to him. The bottle was dripping with moisture. Apparently the bartender had a way of keeping it cool. Gabe reached for the bottle, noticed that the cap had already been removed. The bartender was reaching for a glass. "Never mind," Gabe said. "I'll drink it right out of the bottle."

The two men at the table were now standing up, both of them looking straight at Gabe. He casually looked off to one side. The two men walked toward him, stopped six feet away. The one called Hank was a little to Gabe's right, standing a couple of feet from the bar. The other man leaned against the bar, laying his right hand on its scarred and pitted surface. Gabe recognized him from yesterday; he was the one who'd been about to shoot Hans. The one who'd shouted a threat as he and the other three gunmen had ridden away after Gabe had humiliated them. "Didn't think you was ever gonna see us again, did you, mister?"

Gabe picked up the bottle of root beer with his right hand, put it to his lips, took a sip. Sweetness filled his mouth, mixed with the slight sharpness of herbs. He took another sip. Wonderful.

Hank was chuckling. "Hey, Charlie," he said. "You four yahoos let this one man buffalo you? Hell, he cain't even look us in the eye. Scared shitless."

Charlie, stung, took his right hand from the bar. "Hey, asshole," he said to Gabe, his voice ugly with anger. "We're talkin' to you. Wanna know if you got anything to say 'fore I blow a hole in you."

Gabe saw Charlie's right hand drifting toward the gun he wore on his right hip. Too bad the man was choosing gunplay. Gabe did not want to kill them, that would up the stakes way too high. Killing begat killing. But if Charlie made a move for his pistol . . .

Hank changed the situation. He stepped closer to Gabe, cutting partly in front of Charlie. "Let's not make it too quick, Charlie," Hank said, grinning. "Maybe a little horsewhippin' first. I—Hey!"

Gabe, after a final big swig, swung the root beer bottle at Hank's face. Hank tried to raise a hand to ward off the blow, but he was too late. The bottle thudded into his cheekbone. The bottle did not break, but root beer and blood flew. Stunned, Hank staggered backward.

Gabe leaped forward, pushed Hank into Charlie. Charlie, to keep his balance, slapped his right hand down onto the bar. Hank was still falling when Gabe reached inside his buffalo coat with his left hand and seized the handle of his knife. He ripped the knife free of its sheath, with the blade protruding from the bottom of his fist, alongside his forearm. He slammed his fist down, driving the blade through Charlie's hand, pinning it to the bar. Charlie screamed in agony, stared down at his bloody, impaled hand.

Gabe leaped past him, clubbed Hank on the side of the neck as he went down. When Hank hit the dirty, tobacco-stained barroom floor, he hit like a corpse. Gabe bent, plucked Hank's pistol from its holster, tossed it across the room. It came to rest under a table.

He turned toward the bar. The bartender had backed away, wanting no part of the trouble. Charlie, his face white with pain and fear, was tugging at the knife handle with his left hand, trying to pull it free, but it was sunk deep into the wood. He saw Gabe approaching. Teeth bared, he tried to reach across his body with his left hand, to get to his pistol. Gabe laid his right hand on the butt of his own pistol. "Try it and you're dead."

Gabe's voice was not loud, but the flat menace of it caused Charlie to jerk his hand away from his pistol. He looked down at the knife pinning his hand to the bar. "That was a dirty trick, mister," he whined.

Gabe looked straight at Charlie, who quickly looked away, unable to face the coldness in those gray eyes. He was sure he saw his own death there. Gabe stepped closer. "This is no game," he said quietly. "I came here for a purpose. To warn you. To warn all of you."

"W-warn us about what?" Charlie asked, his voice shaky. The pain in his hand was shooting up into his arm like bolts of electricity.

"About the people who live around here," Gabe replied. "The farmers. If you and your friends keep harassing them, if you hurt any of them at all, I'll have to kill you. Do you understand that? I'll kill every one of you."

The use of the future tense emboldened Charlie; apparently death was not imminent. "You and who else, mister? We work for a big man. He'll plow you under like you was weeds."

Gabe said nothing for a moment. He stepped back a little. "But that'll be too late for you and your friends, won't it?" he said softly. "Because by then, you'll all be dead."

Charlie was about to reply, but his voice rose in a howl of agony as Gabe reached out and took hold of the handle of his knife. To work it out of the bar top, he had to wriggle it back and forth. Charlie reached out with his left, to halt the agonizing sawing motion that was enlarging the wound in his hand, but by then the knife had been freed.

Gabe picked up a bar rag and cleaned the blood from the knife's blade. Charlie was hanging onto the bar, weak and sick with pain. He watched as the man who'd maimed and humiliated him put the knife away beneath the big black coat he was wearing.

Suddenly, there were sounds of shouting from outside, of boots pounding toward the saloon. Gabe figured that the other gunmen must have heard the commotion, or perhaps someone had seen what was happening and had warned them. Gabe turned and began to walk toward the rear door. "Remember what I said," he told Charlie as he passed him. "If you keep molesting innocent people, you'll die. All of you."

"Yeah?" Charlie gritted from between clenched teeth. "You're the one who's gonna die, mister."

By then, Gabe was at the rear door. He turned the knob. Charlie's voice pursued him. "Just tell me your name, shithead," Charlie shouted. "So's we'll know what to put on your tombstone!"

Gabe opened the door, paused in the doorway, turned to face Charlie. "My name?" he asked. "Long Rider will do. Just remember what I warned you about, and you'll never have to hear it again."

CHAPTER SIX

By the time the first of the approaching men rushed through the front door of the saloon, Gabe was out the back door. A quick tug on the slipknot he'd tied earlier freed his horse's reins. He was up in the saddle and riding away into the dark when the back door crashed open and three men ran outside. They had only a glimpse of Gabe, then a moment later he vanished into the darkness, only the sound of his horse's hooves giving away his position. Shots crashed out as two of the three men fired wildly into the night. Gabe looked back, saw pinpoints of reddish-yellow flame. Yes, amateurs, firing blind, and in the process, giving away their own position.

He did not hurry, although he was a little surprised a few minutes later to hear sounds of pursuit behind him. Davis's hired guns had been quick in saddling up their mounts.

A half-moon was just rising in the east, poking up through a gap in the hills that surrounded the town. Riding uphill, Gabe was visible for a moment as he crossed a patch of bare ground. "There he goes," a distant voice called out from behind him.

Gabe was annoyed. He was going to have to lose these clowns. His annoyance helped him decide to teach them a lesson. He was currently riding up a steep path. A couple of hundred yards ahead, the path disappeared into a thick stand of timber. He spurred his horse forward. Once inside the timber, it was very dark; the moonlight, still weak, could not penetrate.

Gabe picked a point where two sturdy trees flanked the sides of the trail. It was a minute's work to string his lariat across the trail, the ends anchored to the trees. Checking to make sure that the rope was almost invisible, he forced his horse off the trail into underbrush, then circled back along the trail, to a point about forty yards from the rope.

Minutes later, four men came pounding along hell-for-leather in single file, taking, in Gabe's estimation, few precautions against ambush. The first two men ran straight into the tautly stretched rope. The leading rider was plucked right out of the saddle, emitting a strangled grunt as the rope dug into his chest just below his throat. The second man, slowed by the fall of the man ahead, hit the rope with less force, but he, too, was unhorsed. The other two riders, unable to get around the frightened, neighing horses of the two fallen men, milled around uncertainly, calling out excited questions. "What the hell happened? You find the bastard?"

Sitting his horse just off the trail, Gabe became aware of another rider approaching. With his eyes somewhat accustomed to the gloom, he saw one man pounding up the trail, a latecomer, who, when he sensed the confusion ahead, reined in his horse. "Hey!" he bellowed. "What the hell's goin' on?"

"Ah, shut up, Jed," a voice called back. "The bastard suckered us."

Jed had pulled up his horse about thirty yards behind the others, just a few feet from where Gabe was waiting, slightly off the trail. Before Jed could urge his horse forward to join the others, Gabe urged his stallion out onto the trail. Jed was unaware of him, until Gabe was only an arm's length away. "Hey!" Jed shouted, starting to reach for his pistol.

But Gabe already had his Winchester out. He slammed the barrel against the side of the gunman's head. Jed grunted, reeled in the saddle, and started to fall. Gabe slipped his Winchester back into its scabbard, caught Jed, and pulled his body across his stallion's withers. Jed lay like a sack of oats, tiny quivers running through his unconscious body. Knowing he would not be out for long, Gabe leaned forward, took a rope from Jed's saddle, then rode back down the trail, toward the town.

It took the other men a few minutes to figure out that Jed had disappeared. They'd heard him cry out, but at first they'd thought he was simply adding to the general din of confusion and anger . . . until they found his riderless horse. "Jeez," one of them muttered. "You s'pose that hombre got him?"

"It weren't the boogeyman," another said sourly. "Guess he got around behind us."

"So what do we do? Head back toward town?"

There was no immediate answer. They were beginning to realize that, out here in the night, they were considerably at the mercy of the spooky son of a bitch who'd already torn the hell out of two of their number in the saloon. "Yeah," one of the men finally said. "We'll see if we can track him, first light."

The others, relieved, pulled their horses around and headed at a slow walk back toward town, leading Jed's horse, muttering bravely about what they were gonna do to the bastard in the morning.

A mile further along, a lone oak grew up beside the trail, old and immense. About eight feet up, one of its limbs overhung the trail. That's where they found Jed hanging. "Goddamn!" one of the men called out. All of them pulled up their horses.

In this more open area, the moonlight was brighter. It was easy to see Jed, slowly swinging back and forth, his hands limp at his sides. Obviously, he'd been hoisted up not long before. His fellow gunmen sat their horses, stunned. "The dirty son of a bitch," one muttered. A slow anger was building inside them. Anger and fear. Each of them had a terror of hanging, a not unlikely fate, considering their chosen profession. To see one of their number strung up right in front of them . . .

Suddenly, a deep moan issued from Jed's gently swaying figure. One of the men backed his horse away, the hair rising on the nape of his neck. Another of the gunmen, one with a little sharper intellect, called out, "Damn! He's still alive! Let's cut him down!"

Since the butt end of the hanging rope had been tied around the tree's trunk, it was a simple matter for one of the men to lean down out of the saddle and cut it. Unfortunately, the rope slipped out of his hands under the weight of Jed's now unsupported body, and Jed fell, hitting the ground with a meaty thud.

The men immediately dismounted. Two of them knelt over Jed. Only then did they realize that the rope had been tied under his arms, instead of around his neck. And only then did they notice the white square of paper tacked to the front of his shirt by the blade of Jed's own knife.

This new discovery diverted attention from Jed, who, recovering consciousness, was beginning to moan louder, his right hand reaching up to a smear of blood at the side of his head. One man tried to read the note by the light of the moon, but could not quite make out the letters. He couldn't read very well anyhow. Finally, another man struck a match, leaned forward, scrutinizing the words neatly written across the paper. "A second warning," the note read. "Leave the area, or some of you will die."

The note was signed, "Long Rider."

"Put out that goddamned match!" one of the men hissed, glancing nervously around, into the darkness. "You're making us all targets."

The match was immediately blown out, partly because it had burned down far enough to scorch the fingers of the man holding it, partly out of sudden, paralyzing fear. The son of a bitch could be out there anywhere, looking at them over a pair of rifle sights.

Jed, still semiconscious, was hoisted up into the saddle. A moment later, all of the men were on their way back toward town, each of them looking nervously over his shoulder. "Goddamn," one of them murmured. "What the hell's goin' on?"

Gabe, sitting his horse about two hundred yards away, waited until the last of them had disappeared from sight. Then he rode back along the trail, where he retrieved his lariat. By now he was hungry, but he decided to put some space between himself and the town. He rode up into the hills, finally branching off the main trail onto a track that led up into broken country. Half an hour later he had found a good place to bed down for the night, a small gully, invisible from the trail, with a tiny spring bubbling a thin stream of water out of a sheer rock face.

Dismounting, Gabe built a small fire. He knew the fire was a risk, that anyone determined to hunt him down would be alerted by the smell of it. But he suspected that none of Davis's gunmen would be leaving town tonight.

He heated a can of beans over the fire, then spooned the beans straight out of the can. As he sat eating, he wondered at the way he'd chosen to sign the note he'd left on Jed's shirt. He'd used his Lakota name, Long Rider. As far as Gabe was concerned, his true name.

Not a name he used much among the whites. As he ate his beans, he thought about how he'd gotten the name, his manhood name. About the adventure that had brought him fame among the Lakota. When he was only fourteen years old, fourteen winters as the People said, word had come that a strong column of soldiers would be passing through an area where a village of people friendly to Gabe's Bad Faces were camped. Most of the warriors were out hunting. Gabe, although young, was the one chosen to warn the camp. It had been wintertime. A blizzard had struck just after he set out. He had ridden for days through the bitter cold and wind, going through two horses, but he had been in time to warn the camp. And because of that long ride through terrible weather, he had gotten his manhood name. A name still remembered among surviving Oglala.

And now that name was but again. Why had he chosen to use it? Perhaps because it was a warrior's name, and once again, Gabe felt like a warrior.

A man with two names. Long Rider, Gabe Conrad. A man of two peoples. When his mother had sent him away to the White Man, she'd called him Gabe, after her old friend, the mountain man, Jim Bridger, whom others often called Old Gabe, comparing Bridger, a formidable figure, to the angel, Gabriel. Old Gabe and young Gabe. And now, once again, young Gabe was to be Long Rider.

It was not until after he had eaten the beans, and the fire had burned down, and there were no further signs of pursuit, that Gabe finally spread out his bedroll and lay down. It had been a good day. He hoped he had taught Davis's men a lesson. And without the necessity of killing any of them. He knew that if he killed without the right kind of justification, the type of justification the White Man considered proper, then the law would step in, and he would be a hunted man, with all the weight of the White Man's civilization out for his head. No, it was better to see if he could simply scare them off. Of course, if he could not, then perhaps men would die. And perhaps he would be one of those who died. The odds were not with him. In the meantime, life would be full for a while, the fullness, the immediacy of danger.

Speaking of fullness, and another kind of excitement, as Gabe fell asleep, his mind filled with remembered images of Naomi's naked body, of the half-hidden mysteries concealed by those dark, enigmatic eyes. Yes, life was definitely becoming much more interesting.

CHAPTER SEVEN

In the morning, Gabe chanced another fire. This time he fried bacon on a flat rock, to go with his beans. He would have liked some coffee, but he seldom carried a pot, or anything else that might clank and warn others of his presence.

Not long after sunup, he rode back toward town, keeping to higher elevations, where he could see a considerable distance in any direction. He once again settled down on the spur of rock overlooking the main street. About ten in the morning he saw five of the gunmen ride out, heading toward the wood where he had bushwhacked them the night before. The previous night's occurrences had obviously not taught them a thing. The gunmen milled about in the wood for a while, then finally picked up Gabe's trail. They began to follow his horse's hoofprints, unaware that Gabe himself was now following them.

They were poor trackers. Half an hour later they lost Gabe's trail where he'd branched off up into the mountains. Gabe, knowing which way they were bound to ride, had already circled around them, and lay concealed in brush, not forty yards away, listening to their frustrated chatter. "Hell," one of them said disgustedly. "He could be anywhere up there."

"Maybe he just rode on out o' the area," another opined. "He looked like he was passin' through, the first time we seen him."

"He gave us all them warnin's, though," another volunteered. "Keeps comin' back at us."

"Yeah."

All five of them mulled that over. Finally, they dismounted and sat by the side of the trail. One of them produced a bottle of whiskey from his saddlebags. "Little hair 'o the dawg," he said, his tone quite happy as he raised the bottle to his lips and took a long drink.

"Hey! Don't hog it all!" another man protested. The bottle then made the rounds. Gabe watched, disgusted. Here these men were, on the trail of a man that had already bested them several times, and they were dulling their wits with alcohol. They weren't even watching the trail around them.

The men began to grow garrulous. "Too bad about Charlie's hand," one of them said. "The way that fella stuck his knife right through it, it don't look like old Charlie's ever gonna be able to handle a gun again."

"Not right-handed, anyhow."

There was a moment's silence. "An' Jed, he's got a real swoll-up noggin on him this mornin'. Afore we left, he was just alayin' there, moanin' 'bout how that bastard laid a rifle barrel up alongside his haid kinda real firm-like."

"Uh-huh," another man muttered, rubbing the side of his own head, which bore a healing scab. Indeed, several of them already wore cuts or bruises given to them by Gabe.

The bottle passed around once more. "Well, reckon we're gonna have ta tell Davis 'bout this," one of the men said.

"He's gonna be pissed."

"He's gonna be more than pissed when he finds out we ain't been doin' our job," the man who'd produced the bottle said. "Tell you what, fellas. Me an' Pete, we'll go on back to town, then head out for the county seat, to tell Davis an' his tame sheriff what's been happenin' here. The rest o' you oughta head on out to the Keppler place. They ain't been listenin' real good to what we been tellin' 'em. Burn down their goddamn barn, or somethin'. Then maybe they'll be happy to sell out, while they're still breathin'."

General muttered agreement followed. Two of the men, moving a little more slowly than when they'd started working on the bottle, mounted, then headed back toward town. The other three watched them ride away, then mounted and headed off toward the left, riding slowly.

Gabe worked his way back through the brush, mounted his horse, and followed the three barn burners. The terrain was very brushy; he almost ran into them once from behind, they were lollygaggin' along so slowly. Gabe fell back a little further. He was beginning to grow angry. Barn burners. Or worse. What if the people at the Keppler place decided to fight back? Would they be gunned down? Gabe had no particular love for barns, but he had a very definite aversion to bullies. Another lesson seemed to be in order.

He heard voices ahead, decided that the three men had stopped. He led his horse off the road, dismounted, pulled his Winchester from its saddle scabbard, then carefully worked his way forward through the brush.

The three gunmen had dismounted. Gabe watched one of them produce another bottle from his saddlebags. "Hey! You was holdin' out on us back there!" one of the men said.

The man with the bottle chuckled. "This here little jug'll go a lot further split only three ways."

There was no argument. All of them sprawled out on the ground, then began to pass the bottle back and forth. As usual, the whiskey got them talking. "That there name," one of them said. "The one that hombre told Charlie and Hank in the saloon. The one he signed on that there note. Long Rider. Think I heard a name like that before, few years back."

"Yeah?" one of the man asked, disinterestedly. Most of his attention was focused on the bottle, which was currently moving away from him.

"Yep. Up around Wyoming. Sounds like the same dude. Big guy, wearin' a funny-lookin' coat with a bird painted on it. Eyes like a real bad sky. Shot up a whole outfit one night, took 'em on by hisself and blasted 'em to hell. A regular one-man army."

"Looks kinda like an Injun to me," one of the men replied disdainfully. "Never worried myself much 'bout Injuns."

"Not too many Injuns with light-colored hair an' eyes," the other man retorted. "Course, he don't wear boots like a civilized man, just them moccasins, an' his skin is sure dark. Maybe he's a half-breed."

One of the men was holding the bottle, looking at it sadly. It was clearly empty, but he tipped it upside down to suck out a final drop or two. "Don't matter nohow this mornin'. Let's get to work."

One of the men smiled. "Barn burnin's real hot work. Maybe Keppler's got a bottle or two stashed away. What say we ask him after we burn down his goddamn shitkicker spread?"

"What say we ask him if he's got a good-lookin' daughter that wants to learn some new games?" another cut in, guffawing.

Their light mood was suddenly ruined when the very man they had so recently been discussing stepped out of the brush not ten feet away. The moccasins they had dismissed so scornfully had not made a sound as Gabe approached. Now, there he stood, rifle in hand, his long black coat and high-crowned hat making him look even taller than he was. "Oh, Jesus!" one of the gunmen yelped. Jumping to his feet, he reached for his pistol.

Gabe was already moving. He stepped in fast, smashed the barrel of his rifle down against the man's gun hand. The man wailed in pain as his pistol fell to the ground. Gabe stepped in closer, reversed his rifle, slammed the butt against the man's jaw.

The man was still falling when Gabe reversed his rifle once again. The other two men were now on their feet, one just behind the man Gabe had felled with his rifle, the other a couple of feet further back. Gabe pulled back the hammer of his rifle. The man closest to Gabe raised his hands well out to the sides, screamed, "Don't shoot! I ain't goin' for it!"

But Gabe jerked his rifle higher and aimed. The man screamed again, folding his crossed arms over his face, staggering backward, unaware that it was not he whom Gabe was aiming at, but the man behind him, who already had his pistol out and was cranking back the hammer.

Gabe shot this third man through the shoulder, his gun-hand shoulder. The man grunted, spun around, began to fall, his pistol spinning away from nerveless fingers, while the man in front of him whimpered at the sound of the shot and folded almost double until he began to realize he had not been hit. Gabe stepped forward, rammed the barrel of his rifle hard into the man's guts. He "oomphed" out a tortured grunt, doubled up again, and slowly folded down onto his knees, his arms wrapped around his stomach.

Gabe stepped past him, stood looking down at the man he'd shot through the shoulder. The man was lying on his back, his eyes partially unfocused from the shock of being shot. Gabe kicked his pistol several yards away. He then turned back to the man he'd hit in the belly, who was still kneeling. Gabe used the sole of his moccasin to push him over onto his side. "You haven't been listening," he said, his voice cold, deadly. "I warned you to leave the farmers alone. I warned you what would happen. Do you understand a little better now?"

"Yeah," the man whimpered. He flinched as Gabe swung the rifle barrel toward him. "No! Don't do it! I hear ya talkin', mister!"

To the man's great relief, Gabe let the rifle hang down at his side. "Take your friends back to town. Tell them what I told you. Tell the others, too. Tell this man who pays you, this Davis, that if he continues to harass people, I'll come for him next. Wherever he is."

The man stared at Gabe blankly. "Did you hear me?" Gabe snapped. "Are you very, very sure that you understand everything I've said?"

The gunman had struggled back up onto his knees. He dared not look Gabe in the eyes. "Yeah. Yeah, mister. I'll tell 'em all."

Gabe looked down at the groveling gunman. He hated cowards. More than hated them. He felt consumed with a raging contempt whenever he met one. Among the People, no one was more despised than a coward. A coward was a danger to the survival of the entire group.

Gabe thought about shooting the man. The Oglala considered it a kindness to kill a coward, to put out of his misery any man who so debased himself. How could any coward bear to live?

But Gabe had spent too much time among white men, had learned too much of their logic. He had softened. He would give this man a chance. He turned and started to walk away, then turned back. "You still have your gun," he said, jerking his chin toward the pistol on the man's hip. "I hope you'll try to use it. It would please me very much to kill you."

Gabe turned his back and walked back toward the brush, with his rifle hanging loosely at his side. The gunman, still on his knees, watched him go. Hate began to tighten the man's resolve. How he'd like to put a slug right in the middle of that bastard's back, that son of a bitch who called himself Long Rider.

The man's hand crept down toward the handle of his pistol. Then he remembered Long Rider's eyes, the cold killing light he'd seen in them, and he knew that if he touched his gun he would die. His hand fell away from his pistol, and he remained hunched on his knees, consumed inside by warring tides of hatred and fear, while he stared at the bright colors of the bird painted on the back of the stranger's coat as he disappeared into the brush.

CHAPTER EIGHT

Gabe sat his horse in a copse of trees about two hundred yards from the Karstedt farm. Everything looked quiet, but he had to make certain; he had already been publicly associated with the Karstedts; there could be a welcoming committee waiting.

It was late afternoon. It had been several days since Gabe had had his confrontation with Davis's gunmen. He'd stayed in the hills, always on the move, keeping away from the farm, not wanting to draw attention to the Karstedts. Perhaps by now any chance of repercussions might have blown over. Still, it was better to be very careful.

A moment later, Gabe saw Hans come out of the house, carrying a bucket of slop toward the pigpen. There seemed to be nothing strained or unnatural about the way he moved, so Gabe nudged his horse forward and rode into the farmyard.

The moment Hans saw movement at the edge of the trees, he looked up sharply and started to turn toward the house. Gabe had already noticed a shotgun leaning against the front doorjamb. But when Hans saw it was Gabe, he relaxed and smiled.

Hans had emptied the bucket into the hog trough by the time Gabe reached him. Hans started to reach up a welcoming hand, then realized it was slimy from the garbage and wiped it on his trouser leg. "We were wondering what happened to you," Hans said. "Actually, we were worried. You might have been lying dead up in some canyon."

Gabe smiled. "Not quite yet," he said, then swung down from his horse.

The sound of Gabe's arrival had penetrated into the house. Eva came out onto the front stoop, followed by Naomi. Gabe watched the girl dry her hands on her apron and stand, watching him. She made no move off the stoop, but he noticed that her eyes were watching him intently. He could not read her expression.

Hans's voice diverted his attention from Naomi. "Come on in. But maybe you'd better put your horse in the barn first."

Gabe had been about to attach his horse's bridle to a post, but the urgency in Hans's voice intrigued him. "Why in the barn?" he asked.

Hans seemed surprised. "You don't know?"

"Know what?"

"About the warrant," Hans replied. "We heard about some of the things you did to Davis's men. The whole county has heard, and Davis's sheriff has sworn out a warrant for your arrest. For attempted murder."

Gabe felt annoyance. He'd stopped himself from killing men who needed killing, men who were bullies and cowards, so that he could avoid trouble with the law. Apparently it had not worked. He considered remounting and riding away, out of this county. Then he turned his head and looked toward where Naomi was standing. She still had not moved, her body betrayed nothing at all, but now he was sure he was able to read desire in her eyes. Reason enough to stay. He led his horse toward the barn, with Hans following.

Once inside the barn, while he removed his horse gear from the stallion's back, Gabe said to Hans, "Perhaps I should ride on. With this warrant, I could cause you trouble by staying."

Hans flushed. "You'll do no such thing! We'll have plenty of trouble whether you stay or not. And after what you've done for us . . ."

As before, when he and Hans headed for the house, Gabe carried both rifles with him. Inside he leaned the rifles against the wall and first took Eva's hand, then Naomi's. The girl's skin was hot to the touch, and now, this close, there was no mistaking the barely controlled excitement in her eyes. Gabe had to force himself to look away.

Eva took charge. "You'll be hungry," she said to Gabe. Then, turning toward the girl, she said, "Naomi, let's start some biscuit batter."

While the women busied themselves in the kitchen, Hans led Gabe into the living room, where he motioned Gabe to a chair, taking one opposite him. "You sure tore those men to pieces," Hans said with evident glee. "Two of them are hurt too badly to do anything but lie in bed. Some of the others were ready to leave the territory."

"However, it sounds like they didn't," Gabe said quietly.

Hans shook his head, and now he looked a little less happy. "No, they decided not to. I suppose some of them were beginning to wonder if what they were up against was worth the money Davis is paying them. But it put some backbone into them when the sheriff issued the warrant. And Davis hired four new men. I saw a couple of the new ones when I went into town the other day. They're much harder-looking than the others. I don't know what it would take to frighten them."

"So then," Gabe said, "nothing has really been accomplished, has it?"

Hans vehemently disagreed. "That's not true! The people around here, people like me and Eva, they feel better now that they see there are ways to stop Davis's men, to hurt them. It'll be harder for Davis to force people to sell. . . ."

"Oh, really?" Naomi said, stepping out of the kitchen, her hands white with flour. "All this new confidence you're talking about, this idea of standing up to Davis, what good does it do? Gabe stood up to Davis's men, and what did it get him? He's a wanted man now."

Hans nodded uncomfortably. "Yes. Davis has not given up. I suppose there will always be lots· of men available, like the ones he hires."

"And not too many to stand up to them," Naomi said scornfully. "That's what it would take. All of us together, standing up to them."

Hans looked at the girl, his face hard. "Davis's men are hired

killers, Naomi. We are farmers. Remember what happened to
Joshua Williams and his son when they tried to run those men
off their farm?"

Naomi bit her lip, looked down. Eva stepped next to the
girl. "They died, Naomi. Killed like cattle. They never stood
a chance."

"But Naomi's right," Gabe said. "Only people working
together stand any real chance. And then, only if they have
power on their side. Legal power. Otherwise, you'll get picked
off, one by one."

"What do you mean?" Hans asked.

"When I was here before, you said that an election for sheriff
is coming up. How soon?"

"Why . . . in a week or so. . . ."

"That's what you need! Your own sheriff. I remember Naomi
mentioning a name."

"Tom," Naomi interjected. "Tom Olafson. He'd make a
good sheriff. He was in the war, he got a medal. He's a
brave man."

"But," Eva protested, "bravery might not be enough. If he
became a candidate, I'm sure something bad would happen to
him. Some . . . accident."

"It can be done," Gabe insisted. "But it all depends on
timing. If the election were more than a week away, perhaps
it would be impossible. There'd be too much time for that
'accident' to happen. But in only a week . . . Do you think
people would vote for this man?"

"Yes," Hans said. "I think almost everyone would vote for
Tom."

Gabe looked straight at Hans. "But would they fight for
him?"

"Aaahhhh." Hans gave a very European shrug, hands out
to the side, palms up. "That I do not know. Perhaps if they
thought they had a good chance of winning. . . ."

Naomi stepped forward, her face shining with youthful zeal.
"Yes, they might fight. I see what you mean, Gabe, about it
being important that there's only a week to the election. It
won't give Davis much chance . . ."

"Uh-huh," Gabe finished for her. "If it's done right, he'll be taken by surprise. Oh, he'll probably try something, but if any counter moves he makes are stopped quickly, he won't have time to think up new ones."

The Karstedts began talking animatedly among themselves. They were suddenly in the midst of planning an election campaign. Gabe sat silently, listening, watching. They had so much enthusiasm, although they didn't even know for certain that this man, Tom Olafson, would run for sheriff. Their enthusiasm proved once again to Gabe how much they wanted to keep their land. If some of their neighbors were as committed as the Karstedts, then there might be a chance. An outside chance. He wondered if, in their new enthusiasm, they would adequately weigh the dangers. Some of them might die. But he would do his best to see that they did not.

The day was coming to a close. Eva saw Gabe looking outside at the lengthening shadows. "We must make you up a place to sleep," she said. "Not the barn this time. Naomi can sleep in with us. You'll have her room."

Gabe shot a quick look at Naomi, saw a flash of alarm and disappointment in her eyes as she thought of being locked in with her grandparents, away from Gabe. "I don't think that's a good idea," Gabe replied. "I'm a wanted man. If someone came here . . ."

"Ridiculous!" Hans said. "After all you've done for us, if we can't stick our own necks out a little . . ."

Gabe smiled. "It's not that. If they do come, I'd be trapped inside the house."

"Well, yes, I suppose so," Hans said grudgingly. "The barn, then."

Gabe shook his head. "Not that either." He could see himself, in the back stall, his horse unsaddled, men surrounding the barn, bursting in through the doorway, perhaps burning him out. "I'll make camp somewhere."

"I know just the place," Naomi said, her eyes dancing. "In a little meadow, just a few hundred yards from the house. It's very hard to find."

"Ah yes," Eva said somewhat testily. "Your secret place."

"Very secret," Naomi replied combatively. "Just what Gabe needs. After all, you've never found it, have you?"

She turned back toward Gabe. "I better show you where it is before it gets too dark."

She moved toward the door, looked back questioningly at Gabe. Gabe looked over at Hans and Eva. Both seemed a little confused. "Well . . ." Hans muttered. Eva looked from Gabe to Naomi. The girl's face was a giveaway, flushed and excited, impatient.

Eva sighed. "Go," she said. "But Naomi," and now her voice was stern. "You be back here before dark."

Gabe started to follow Naomi. Eva stopped him. "I have some pie," she said. "Take it with you."

She went into the kitchen, came back with half a pie. Cherry, Gabe saw. He took it, thanked Eva. Naomi was already outside, waiting by his horse. He mounted, balanced the pie on the pommel of his saddle, then leaned down, offering Naomi his hand. She took it and swung up behind him.

As they rode away, Gabe saw that Eva and Hans were standing on the front porch, watching them go. Both looked a little sad. Naomi waved.

Naomi guided Gabe away from the house, up a gentle slope. A thick wood lay ahead. "It's in there," Naomi said. "But from outside, you can't see anything."

They rode around in a loop, Naomi explaining that you could only come at the place from behind. A trail led off to one side. They followed it for a while, then Naomi pointed to a barely imperceptible break in the bushes alongside the trail. "In there," she said.

The bushes parted easily. Within fifty yards a small clearing opened out ahead of them, sunk into a low spot. A tiny stream ran along one side. Trees grew up all around the clearing, which was floored in grass and flowers. "This is it," Naomi said.

Gabe smiled. "Your secret place."

She nodded behind him, then slid off the horse. Gabe swung down too, stood facing her, awkwardly balancing the pie. "And what kind of secret things do you do here?" he asked the girl.

She stood about two feet away, looking up at him. Her eyes were big, dark, eager pools. "Up until now," she murmured, her voice throaty, a little strained, "not nearly enough."

Then she was in his arms. It was difficult, holding the pie behind her back. "Oh, Gabe!" Naomi murmured. "I missed you so much! When we heard about all the trouble, and the warrant, I was so worried, so scared. And now . . . here you are. And I can't wait. . . ."

Her breasts were pressing hard against Gabe's chest. He could feel her body trembling. This was not the time for more talking, not even the time for a kiss. Definitely not the right time for pie. Gabe dropped the pie onto the grass behind Naomi, then began to fumble with her clothing, swearing at unfamiliar buttons and hooks. Laughing happily, Naomi helped him. When they'd unbuttoned the top of the dress, she simply let it slide down over her hips. She now wore only a light chemise, a simple, thin, white garment. She reached down, took hold of the hem, pulled the chemise up over her head. To Gabe, it was like unveiling a wonderful work of art.

When it was over, they lay beside each other for several minutes. Then Naomi began to wriggle beneath Gabe. "Oooohhhh . . . my back itches . . . the grass."

Gabe got up, went over to his horse, and unrolled his bedroll. There was a loose blanket inside. He laid it on the ground. Naomi rolled over onto it. Gabe saw how the grass had been flattened where they'd made love, saw a couple of clumps of grass he'd torn up with his hands during their lovemaking, when it had seemed as if he were going to explode.

He lay down on the blanket, next to Naomi. She snuggled against him. Her skin was hot, a little damp. "I thought you would never come back."

"But I did," he replied.

She nodded, but her expression was sad. "Yes. This time."

He said nothing. Suddenly, Naomi rolled over onto her back and laughed. "Now I really do have a secret for this place."

Gabe looked at her, at her expression of innocent pleasure. Perhaps she had more than just this one secret. As she had said the first time they'd made love, she had not come to him as a virgin. Which he preferred. He'd long ago discovered, ruefully, that virgins could be a great deal of trouble; they were certainly a lot of responsibility. Some virgins cried, some half-died of shame after their passion was spent, some were delighted with their new status. Like Naomi; she seemed to be delighted each time he made love to her, as if it were the first time, as if the pleasure and excitement of it was eternally new, as if it was totally unexpected.

She draped an arm over him, began to stroke his chest. "When I get back to the house," she murmured into his shoulder, "Eva will know. Just by looking at me."

Looking down at the girl's flushed face, at that expression worn only be women who have just made love, Gabe had no doubt that she was right. "What do you think she'll do?" he asked.

Naomi shrugged. "Not much. She'll just look at me kind of funny, like the time before."

"And Hans?"

"Oh, he might know, too, but he won't let himself really think about it. Grandfathers can be funny, sometimes. I suppose fathers might be, too. I don't know. I can't remember mine. Hans and Eva are all I've ever known. I would never want to hurt them, but . . . how could I ever think of living without this? Without making love?"

Gabe had been remembering his own adventures with a number of irate fathers. Now he thought about what she had just said. Yes, how to live without making love? One could exist, of course, but not really live, not really be alive. Life without a woman's warmth was bare, hungry survival.

"I never knew it could be so good," Naomi said. "Everybody should know how good it can be, then there would never be any more unhappiness. Not anywhere in the whole, wide world."

Gabe laughed. "Perhaps. If every woman enjoyed it the way you do."

She pushed her body upward, looked down at him, surprise on her face. "They don't?"

He shook his head. "No. You're . . . exceptional."

She beamed with pleasure. "Somebody else told me that once." Then her eyes widened in embarrassment. "Oops," she said, putting a hand over her mouth.

Gabe laughed. "That man knew what he was talking about."

Her eyes were still wide, apprehensive. "You're not jealous?"

He shook his head again. She beamed with delight. Then her face clouded. "You're not jealous because you just don't care."

He groaned. "Stop it!" He pulled her down to him, kissed her. She seemed surprised for a moment, then kissed him back.

When they broke apart, he saw tears on her cheeks. "For now," she said. "For now, while we have each other."

Gabe did not know what to reply. He looked around, saw that it was beginning to grow dark. Naomi noticed it, too. "Oh, Eva will . . ."

She rolled free, slipped into her shift. Gabe pointed. "No underwear?" he observed.

She grinned. "Remember when I went into my room for a few minutes? While Eva was bringing out dinner? I took my bloomers off, so I would be more . . . ready."

Gabe laughed. Naomi flushed. He lay on the blanket, watching her put on her dress. She looked around quickly, at the darkness invading the trees, then bent low, kissed him quickly. "Bye," she said, then started away, nearly skipping in her happiness.

Gabe watched her disappear into the thick bushes that screened the little glade, then he lay back again on his blanket, aware of many sensations. For just a moment he experienced a touch of unease, wondering if he would end up hurting the girl badly someday. He discounted it. Not Naomi; she was one of the ones who knew what she wanted, and took it. Yes, she might be sad for a while, but he had long ago discovered that women usually recovered from broken hearts much more easily than men. Women, the more practical sex, the ones who thought about the future, about security. For the moment, Naomi was in the middle of an adventure. Later . . . who knew?

His hand fell to one side, touched something sticky. The pie. He reached out for it, and as he ate, he was certain of one thing. In Naomi, he now had something worth fighting for, something that made him happy to stay for a while.

Yes, fighting partly because of a woman. What a fool I am, he thought. Like all men.

But when he finally fell asleep, there was a satisfied smile on his face.

CHAPTER NINE

Gabe remained in Naomi's little glade until mid-morning, when hunger finally drove him to the house. He'd awakened at first light, listening to the world wake with him, small animals scurrying through the grass and bushes, birds singing to the sun, the drone of insects. He lay on his back in his bedroll, looking up at the sky, light blue and cloudless. His body was relaxed, his memories of the night before pleasant. He smiled. He was a very lucky man, no one's slave, free to go where he chose, and now, for the moment, not at all lonely.

He washed in the little stream, then dressed and strapped on his weapons. He debated saddling his horse, but decided to leave it where it was; there was plenty of grass, and it would not be spotted by anyone who rode up to the house.

He realized that Naomi's little glade was really not very far from the house. He and the girl had ridden around the long way. It took Gabe only a few minutes to find a more direct route through the bushes and trees, although he had to get down on all fours at one point and slip under some particularly thick bushes.

He could smell the house before he reached it, good smells, coffee, bacon, bread. He stopped at the edge of a thicket, studying the house, looking for signs of anything wrong, of unwanted company. Finally, satisfied, he stepped into the open, but his Winchester was ready in his right hand.

He had nearly reached the front porch when Naomi came outside, briskly wielding a broom. She did not see him until he was only a few feet away. She looked up, startled at first, even a little frightened, then, as she recognized him, she smiled, a slow, beautiful, satisfied smile. My God, girl, he thought, if you go around looking that way, absolutely everyone will know what we've been doing.

Naomi dropped her broom. "Come in. The bacon is still warm. I'll fry you some eggs."

Eva was in the kitchen, washing pots. When Gabe came inside, she turned and looked at him appraisingly, almost coolly. Obviously, she knew. She looked from Naomi to Gabe, and back to Naomi again. Perhaps it was the look of pure happiness on the girl's face that decided Eva. Perhaps it was memories of her own youth. She smiled at Naomi, a warm, accepting smile. The girl flushed, then left the room, flustered. Gabe heard the sound of sweeping start up again.

Eva turned toward Gabe. "She has never been an easy child to control," she said, looking down at the pan she was washing. "Not that we ever cared to control her, she is not a machine, nor an animal."

Now she turned to face Gabe. "I don't think you will do anything to harm her."

Gabe nodded, a little embarrassed. Eva turned back to the sink. "Who knows?" she murmured. "More likely, she might do the harming. Naomi goes after what she wants. And she usually gets it."

A few minutes later, Naomi came back into the kitchen and began energetically making breakfast. Within ten minutes, Gabe was eating the usual big Karstedt meal, in this case, bacon and eggs, biscuits with gravy, coffee, and a slice of fried meat.

Gabe had already noticed that Hans was absent. "He's gone to talk to Tom Olafson," Eva told him when he asked. "Left at dawn."

After breakfast, there was little for Gabe to do. He sat on the porch, watching the women go about their seemingly endless chores: cleaning the house and its utensils, preparing and preserving food, mending clothing, drawing water, making small repairs that Hans would not bother with. An unending routine. No wonder a young woman like Naomi, with her bright, quick mind, would be eager to search out adventure. No wonder women aged so quickly. At least, the ones who spent their days as these women did. Gabe had seen spoiled, aristocratic women in the East. No quick aging for them.

Gabe leaned back against the wall, aware of the house behind him, the barn ahead, the corral, animal pens, and small outbuildings scattered here and there. Sitting quietly, with time to think, he felt all the various structures around him as a vast weight. He tried to imagine actually owning all these things, the buildings, animals, gear. He could not, could only think of them as a terrible weight, as a chain that would bind a man immobile. Once again, he was thankful for his lack of impedimenta, thankful to be free to move on when he wished.

Naomi had read him correctly. One day, he would ride away. That was his nature. And, watching Naomi, watching the way she looked at all these objects that went with the farm, he realized that this was her nature, to have home, family, beloved belongings, all those things that meant stability, permanence. As if there actually was any permanence to a human life, other than life itself. And the permanence of death, of course, life's alter ego.

Gabe was still sitting on the front porch in the late morning, honing the blade of his knife and spinning grand thoughts, when Hans rode up, accompanied by another man. Gabe watched them dismount, paying particular attention to the newcomer. He was a little above average height, strongly built, with big, work-worn hands. He appeared to be in his late thirties, perhaps even his early forties. Gabe noticed that he was carrying a pistol, worn high on his belt, toward the back. A practical rig, not a gunfighter's.

Hans made the introductions. "Gabe Conrad . . . Tom Olafson."

After the horses had been taken care of, the three men sat on the porch. Eva brought coffee for Tom and Hans, but for Gabe, a special treat. Buttermilk. The coffee and milk ritual gave Gabe and Tom a chance to study one another. Gabe liked what he saw, liked the quiet strength he saw in Tom's face, his economical way of moving. Here was a man who could control himself without being stiff, clumsy.

"I've told Tom about your idea," Hans said to Gabe. "He's interested."

But not eager, Gabe thought. Which was good; this was not a man who craved power for its own sake. "I guess something's gotta be done," Tom finally said. "Or we'll lose everything we worked for, all of us."

The actual planning was fairly simple. Tom would simply ride into the county seat and file for the election. This would not be particularly dangerous, at least, not right away, since Davis's thugs were not headquartered there. Just ride in, register, then ride out. "After that," Gabe said to Tom, "you can never be alone. Not until after the election. If you're ever caught by yourself . . ."

Tom nodded. No false heroics, Gabe decided. A good, steady man. "We'll have to let people know I'm running," Tom said.

It was decided that, as soon as Tom had declared himself, every farmer in the area, the vast majority of the population, would be informed. "And we'll win!" Hans said fiercely.

After the plans had been made, the men relaxed, and the women came out onto the porch. Gabe realized that Tom and the Karstedts must know one another well; there was an easy familiarity between them. He also noticed the many little looks Tom cast in Naomi's direction when he didn't think she was looking. He likes her, Gabe thought. And from the occasional thoughtful look he gave Gabe, Tom was probably wondering about Gabe and Naomi.

No time to worry about that now. It was decided that Tom would return to his farm, ready himself for a morning ride to the county seat. "It ain't too hard for me to do this," Tom said, with just a little bitterness in his voice. "Ain't got much to keep me at home."

Tom left half an hour later, a resolute figure mounted on a fairly decent horse. They all watched him ride away. "A good man," Eva said. "I hope we're not getting him killed."

"Like he said," Hans replied, "he hasn't got much to lose."

Eva saw that Gabe did not understand. "Tom's wife died about six months ago," she said sadly. "There's nobody on his farm now except him. A lonely, sad place. Another man might have left, but not Tom, not as long as his wife's buried on their land."

Hans cut in. "He's always figured that the troubles with Davis helped kill her. She never was a strong woman, and when the threats started to come . . . Well, he has more reasons than most of us to want to fight Davis and the railroad."

Gabe nodded. Now he had a clearer picture of Tom's motivations. Strong motivations. Tom would not fold without a fight.

"I'll start out in the morning," Hans was saying. "Go over to the Smith place. Jack Smith's got three sons who can ride like wild Indians. They can let everyone know that Tom is running for sheriff."

Gabe and Hans spent another hour planning. "I know of at least three men who will ride with you and Tom," Hans told Gabe. "As long as they think there's a chance of us winning. And after the way you already plowed up Davis's men, they'll think there's more than just a chance. And of course, there's me. I'll ride with you, too."

"Hans!" Eva broke in, alarmed. "You'll do no such thing!"

Hans looked at her fiercely. "You think I'm too old, woman?"

"No, but I . . ."

Eva was clearly very distraught. Hans stood up, put an arm around her. "Eva," he said, "in the Old Country I did nothing when the troubles started. I let men very much like the men who work for Davis run us off our property, take away everything we had. Including our pride. I will not let that happen again. Not here, not in this new land."

Gabe sat quietly while Hans and Eva went off to their room, Hans still with his arm around Eva. After the door had shut behind them, he got up from his chair. Naomi was working hard at the churn, making butter. "I'll be back later," he told the girl.

"Do you have to go?" she asked, with just a little petulance in her voice.

"Yes."

He walked away, heading back toward the little glade, taking the long way this time; there was no hurry. Perhaps today would be the last day for a long time in which there would be no sense of hurry, no menace.

When Gabe got back to the glade, he went to his saddlebags and took out a pipe, the kind of pipe the White Man tended to call a peace pipe. Quite erroneously, Gabe reflected. Yes, it was smoked at treaty agreements, when the White Man was present, lying, making promises he would never keep. But the pipes were smoked at other times, too. Whenever a man wanted to feel connected to a power greater than himself.

Gabe's pipe had been given to him many years before, when he'd been in the army jail, given to him by an old Oglala sub-chief and medicine man, Two Face, just minutes before Two Face was taken out to be hanged. More White Man's injustice, Gabe remembered. Two Face, wanting to make peace with the whites, had purchased a captive from the Cheyenne, a white woman named Mrs. Eubanks, with the intention of returning her to her own people as a peace offering. Unfortunately, thinking he would give Mrs. Eubanks a chance to properly thank him for his generous act, in the only way a woman could properly thank a warrior, Two Face had tried to make love to her. She had fought him off, and so he was sentenced to hang for attempted rape.

As the soldiers took Two Face, and his companion, Black Foot, out to be hanged, he had slipped Gabe his ceremonial pipe. He had also given Gabe another gift, a prophecy that Gabe would soon be free, that he would join the People again, that he would become a great man among them. For a little while.

Now, remembering, Gabe ran his hands slowly over the pipe. The bowl had been carved from a special red stone, taken from a quarry in the Lakota's old hunting grounds in western Minnesota. The stone felt warm and smooth against his fingers. The stem was made of a hollowed-out willow branch. Beneath the bowl hung four strips of colored cloth, along with an eagle feather. The cloth strips were there to remind the smoker of the spirits of the four directions, while the eagle feather, a power object much more potent than cloth could ever be, was there to remind one of *Wakan-tanka*, the Great Spirit, that elusive power that lay behind all that existed. The pipe Gabe held in his hands was a thing of power, the pipe of a man of wisdom.

Gabe rummaged further into his saddlebags and pulled out a small pouch of Indian tobacco, *chanshasha*, a mixture of wild tobacco and willow bark. He packed the pipe's bowl with the smoking mixture, then walked across the glade to a spot he'd already picked out, the highest spot in the glade, near a clump of thick bushes. He'd noticed that particular spot shortly after awakening. To him, it was an obvious place of power.

He built a small fire of small pieces of wood that would burn down to very hot coals. He smiled at himself as he struck a match to start the fire. What would Two Face have said to that?

Gabe sat cross-legged in a place that felt exactly right. When the fire had burned long enough and the coals were glowing red, Gabe picked up the pipe, with the bowl in his left hand and the stem in his right. He presented the pipe first to the spirits of the four directions, west, north, east, and south. Then he held the pipe down toward the earth, and finally, up toward the sky.

He gingerly scooped up a coal and dropped it into the pipe's bowl. As the *chanshasha* began to smoke, Gabe placed the pipe to his lips and inhaled, and as the pungent fumes of the smoking mixture filled his lungs, he felt his whole being begin to fill with power, with the power of those strange, ultimately unknowable forces that made up the world. Power to steady his mind, strengthen his body, confirm his resolve.

Gabe smoked until the pipe's bowl was empty. He sat quietly for a while, feeling solid, immovable, as if he grew out of the earth in the way that a tree grew. He was now one with everything around him. He smiled, aware of what the average white man would think if he saw him sitting there, heathen Indian pipe in hand, if he could know of his inner feelings. Superstition, a white man would call it. To Gabe, it was simply reality, a way of connecting to all that lay around him, the great mystery of being, without having to clutter his mind with a distant, intellectualized God, divorced from the world, divorced from creation. Gabe knew much of the White Man's way, of his great civilizations, his towering philosophies, but the old way, the Lakota way, the way of life, was always Gabe's first choice. It was the way of power.

Gabe got up, wiped the pipe bowl clean with a handful of grass, then put the pipe back into his saddlebags. Tomorrow would be a time for action, today, a time for peace. He would take advantage of today, let tomorrow arrive on its own.

He was sitting next to the stream, trailing his hand in cool water, when he heard the sound of someone approaching through the bushes. He turned toward his rifle, which was only a few feet away, then relaxed when he heard a soft curse. "Damn berry bushes!"

The voice was Naomi's. Gabe smiled. It appeared that the rest of the afternoon would be filled with a great deal of activity after all.

CHAPTER TEN

They met in a meadow partway up in the hills, eight of them, Hans, Tom Olafson, Gabe, and five of Tom's supporters, the ones ready to stick their necks out to see Tom elected sheriff. They were meeting in the meadow because Tom's house was considered to be far too dangerous a location. And none of the men cared to bring disaster down on his own house, in case Jethro Davis's men discovered where they were meeting. "They're alayin' for you, Tom," one of the men was saying. "Those yahoos o' Davis's are puttin' out the word all over town . . . that you're gonna be dog meat."

Tom smiled. "Not quite yet."

"They're botherin' people," a man named Josh put in. "They're tellin' 'em if they vote for you, they're dog meat, too."

Tom frowned. "That's more serious. If people don't vote . . ."

"That's why we can't just keep hiding," Gabe said. Until now, he'd been silent, letting the others bring up as many points as possible. "Some of you, like Henry, think we should just keep lying low until the election. Avoid a confrontation."

"Sure. Why ask for trouble?" Henry grumbled. "No point in gettin' shot up."

Gabe studied Henry for a moment. He was a big, heavyset man, with a meaty, expressionless face. Gabe did not think that

Henry was a coward. It was simply that few of these men were fighters by nature. "The idea is for *them* to get shot up, not us," Gabe replied.

"But they're professional gunmen," Henry insisted. "They got the advantage."

Gabe shook his head. "No. We have the advantage. Davis's men are strangers in these parts. You men know the land. You know each other, know your neighbors. You know everything that goes on here. And with that kind of knowledge, you can make things happen your way."

A little life was beginning to come into Henry's heavy features. "Yeah?" he asked. "How?"

"By making them come to us. On our ground."

Gabe turned to Tom. "Tell them what we've been working up."

Tom smiled ruefully. "We?" he asked. "It was your idea, Gabe."

But when Tom turned to speak to the others, the rueful smile was gone. He was all business now, serious, steady. Gabe was a little more certain each day that Tom was the man the locals needed. "Here's what we've worked out," Tom said. He began to talk, and as he talked, smiles began to break out on the faces of the others. Smiles a little tinged by nervousness, but still, smiles.

Early the next morning, before the gunmen had shambled from the hotel, on their way to the saloon, one of the men who'd been with Tom, Gabe, and the others, rode into town. It took him only a few minutes to tack up several posters at prominent points, where the local people would be able to read them.

Since two of the notices had been posted along the route between the hotel and the saloon, Davis's men, when they finally sallied forth to conquer their hangovers, saw the notices, too. "Hey, boys," one of them said after laboriously working his way through daunting, two-syllable words, "it looks like we got the bastards now. Says here that that idiot, Olafson, is gonna give a speech in town today."

One of the others, trying to think past a splitting whiskey

headache, muttered, "Good. We'll put a few holes in the bastard, an' this whole damn thing'll be over."

Another snickered. "Yeah, it'll be easy. We kin just pot him through the saloon doors. Won't even have to get up off our asses."

"Use your head, Alonzo," the first man said. "We cain't just shoot the bastard down in front o' the whole town. Could be trouble down the road. Hell, he's runnin' for sheriff."

"So, whatta we do?" Alonzo asked sourly, casting an anxious look toward the saloon. His body was screaming for a drink. "Are we s'posed to just let him ride inta town, give his goddamn speech, an' ride out? Hell, we might as well vote for the bastard ourselves."

"Uh-uh," the other man said. He pointed toward the poster. "Says here that he's gonna give another speech first, down the road a few miles." The man looked up at the sun. "Hell, he should be talkin' away 'bout now."

"You sorry to be missin' it, Zeke?" one of the other men asked, grinning. "Shit, I think maybe you *are* gonna vote for that farmer."

Zeke scowled. "Trouble with you yahoos, you don't use your noodles. There's only one trail between here an' where Olafson is beatin' his gums right now. Only one way he can ride in here."

Some of the others, despite their morning slowness, were beginning to get Zeke's drift. Smiles began to blossom. "Well, hell, Zeke," one of them said. "How 'bout all of us fellers goin' joggin' on down the trail. We could be kind of like a welcomin' committee for Mr. thinks-he's-gonna-be-sheriff Olafson."

Zeke smiled back. "Yep. Now you're catchin' on. Come on, boys . . . let's ride."

As the others started to turn, to head for the livery stable and their horses, Zeke added cheerfully, "Trouble with most o' you yahoos, you just don't do enough thinkin'. Don't use your brains hardly a'tall. Hell," he added, chuckling, "probably don't *have* no brains."

But, if Zeke had had as much brains, as much awareness as he had mouth, he might have noticed a man slip away from where he'd been standing, just a few feet away, hidden around a corner, and walk quickly to the back of a building, where another man was standing next to a saddled horse. "They took the bait," the first man said. "They'll be riding out in a little while."

The second man nodded, then mounted. He said nothing, not trusting his voice, knowing that, in another hour or so, he could easily be dead. He waved, then turned his horse and rode toward the edge of town, not kicking the animal into a gallop until he knew he was out of hearing. Now the tension inside of him was quickly turning into elated excitement. If he lived, he was going to have a lot to tell his grandchildren.

If he lived.

About five miles from town, the trail narrowed at a point where the river had cut a vee through a low sandstone ridge. It was a perfect place for an ambush. Gabe and Tom had known that if Davis's men took the bait, they'd probably try to ambush Tom there. The point was to ambush the ambushers.

Tom and his party had been waiting near the vee for over an hour when the rider from town came into view, quirting an already lathered horse. "They're on their way!" he called out when he saw the others.

"All right, men," Tom said quietly. "Take cover."

Four of the men, including the messenger from town, took up positions in the brush on either side of the vee. Gabe, Tom, and Henry rode through the vee twice, to make certain the men could not be seen from the trail.

Gabe was surprised that Henry, who had not been anxious to fight the day before, had volunteered for this more hazardous position; the three of them would be out in the open. Hell, Henry had insisted. Tom had gone along with Henry's request. Gabe, feeling Tom probably knew Henry better than he did, said nothing. Together, the three of them rode back down the trail a hundred yards and sat their horses, waiting. One of the men had left the brush and was sprawled on top of the little ridge, watching the trail back toward town. A few minutes later, he waved toward where Gabe, Tom, and Henry were waiting, then he quickly slid back down into the brush.

Tom led the way, riding slowly toward the vee, which

opened out in their direction, narrowing toward the ridge. They were still fifty yards from the notch where the vee narrowed when Davis's men came into sight, riding through the notch at a canter, ready to hide in the brush to set up their ambush. They pulled up hard when they saw the three men riding toward them.

"Whoa, boys," Zeke said. "Only three of them. Not exactly a big turnout. That don't seem right."

He glanced nervously around at the brush, but there was nothing to be seen. By now, Tom and his two companions had stopped about forty yards away, fanned out in a line with about five yards separating each of them.

Zeke forgot the brush, turned to face Tom. "Where you off to, Olafson?" he asked. "Goin' to a funeral?"

"Yeah." Alonzo chuckled. "His own."

By now, one of the gunmen had recognized Gabe. "Gawd!" he burst out. "It's him! It's that goddamn half-Injun!"

The gunmen stared at Gabe. A few automatically backed their horses away. "Hold your ground!" Zeke snarled. He was one of the newcomers; he'd had no personal contact with Gabe, had not yet learned to fear him. Indeed, he had scoffed at the others, accusing them of making up boogeyman stories. Now, face-to-face, Zeke had to admit that, yeah, this Long Rider character was big, and he was sitting his horse steady as a rock, but he was only a man, one of three, facing seven.

Tom nudged his horse forward a little. "You men get out of the way," he said, his voice even, steady. "You're blocking the trail."

Zeke laughed. "You ain't goin' nowhere, Olafson. 'Cept to that funeral Alonzo mentioned. An' you ain't got nobody but yourself to blame. You wouldn't listen, you had to be a big man. Now, you're gonna pay. The men with you are gonna pay, too, lessen they turn and ride away. But not you, Olafson. No ridin' away for you. You've reached the end of your trail."

"I'll have to warn you, mister," Tom said, his voice still steady. "Trying to intimidate a candidate for public office is against the law. Now I'll warn you just once . . . turn around and ride away. Save yourselves a lot of trouble."

Zeke laughed again, but the laugh had less assurance. His attention was diverted when Alonzo called out, "Hell, you ain't sheriff yet, Olafson. An' speakin' o' the law, you're harborin' a fugitive from justice."

He pointed toward Gabe. The men around Alonzo muttered their concurrence. Everyone except Zeke. He was beginning to grow worried. This yahoo, Olafson, should have been shaking in his boots, yet he seemed assured, confident. What did he know that Zeke didn't know? Zeke looked around to the sides, just in time to catch a flicker of movement in the brush, as one of the men hidden there inexpertly tried to move into a better position.

"Look out, boys!" Zeke shouted. "It's a trap!"

Men reached for guns. "Open fire!" Tom yelled, jerking out his own Winchester and spurring his horse forward.

Rifles crashed, tongues of flame burst from the brush, but only one of the gunmen went down in that first wild, poorly-aimed volley. The others started to return the fire, then realized that the three men in front of them were charging; they were caught in a deadly cross fire. They could not ride back the way they'd come, because the narrow notch behind them was now blocked by riflemen. The only way out was straight ahead. Through the three men charging them.

Gabe was positioned to Tom's left, Henry on Tom's right. Gabe saw that the six gunmen still in their saddles were getting ready to charge. No, five; another had been hit by the heavy fire from the brush. Gabe kicked his stallion forward, stood in the stirrups, yelled an Oglala war cry, and charged straight forward, zigzagging his mount with pressure from his knees, firing his rifle from the shoulder.

Bullets were whistling past Gabe's head. A man went down ahead of him. Gabe looked quickly to his right. Tom was riding straight in, with Henry level to his right. The two groups of men were so close now that the riflemen hidden in the brush suddenly stopped firing, afraid of hitting one of their own. Gabe silently cursed; a mistake in tactics. But the imminence of the fight overwhelmed his regrets, and he continued his charge, yelling exultantly.

Gabe's horse barreled into the horse of one of the gunmen.

The impact knocked the Winchester from Gabe's hand. The gunman tried to bring his own rifle around, but the shock of collision had caused him to lose his balance in the saddle. Gabe reached over with his left hand, tugged the pistol from his right hip, and shot the man through the neck. The gunman fell from his horse, choking.

Gabe looked to his right. Tom was right in the middle of the three remaining gunmen, trading shots with one, totally unaware of another of the gunmen, off to the side a few yards, leveling a pistol at Tom's back. Gabe started to bring his pistol up, but his horse, accidentally stepping on the body of the man Gabe had just shot, reared, spoiling Gabe's aim.

It was Henry who saved Tom. Ignoring the bandit to his own right, Henry turned his back on the man and put two bullets from his Winchester into the one who was aiming at Tom. Henry tried to turn back toward the man to his side, but he was too late. The man's rifle roared, and Henry was knocked out of his saddle. Almost instantly, Tom and Gabe fired together, killing the man who'd shot Henry.

Only one of Davis's gunmen remained unwounded. In the confusion after Henry went down, realizing that the fight was lost, that all his companions had been hit, the man wheeled his horse and made a break for it, right back through the vee, right through the ambush. After a moment's surprise, the men hidden in the brush, most of whom had stood up by now, opened fire, but the fugitive, lying flat along his horse, made it through unscathed. Once through the gap, he was safe. As the firing died down, the sound of his horse's hooves could be heard, fading away into the distance.

The riflemen came pouring out of the brush. Gabe noticed that one of them had a patch of blood on his side; another of the men was helping him along. From the way he was walking, he was not too badly hit.

Henry was another matter. Tom had dismounted and was kneeling by him. Gabe rode over close, dismounted, and looked over Tom's shoulder.

Henry had been hit low in the side. Blood was slowly welling out. If the bullet had passed through Henry's intestines, well . . .

Henry's face was twisted in pain, but he smiled when he saw
Tom bending over him. "We took 'em, Sheriff, didn't we?" he
whispered.

"Yeah, we took 'em," Tom replied. He was staring at Henry's wound. "But it won't be worth it, nothing would be worth
it if . . ."

Gabe put his hand on Tom's shoulder. "You picked a good
man to have ride in with us," he said.

Henry heard him and smiled again. "Thanks," he said. Then
he passed out.

Tom was struggling to regain control of himself. "I'm not
used to this kind of thing," he said. "Hope I never do get
used to it."

He visibly steadied himself, turned to his men, began issuing
orders. Three men were sent to cut saplings, to make a travois
for Henry. One of the men, with experience doctoring horses,
bound up Henry's wound. A quick count showed two of the
gunmen still alive, although they'd been wounded badly. More
travois would have to be cut. Through it all, Gabe noticed that
Tom appeared cool, decisive. But from time to time Tom
glanced over at where Henry was lying, and every time he
did, his face pinched inward.

Some of the others were showing signs of queasiness. The
smell of blood hung in the air, mixed with a few lingering
whiffs of powder smoke. Horses were nickering nervously,
the two wounded gunmen were groaning loudly. Few of the
victors were used to fighting, to killing.

As they got ready to ride toward town, with the wounded
loaded onto the travois, Tom rode over to Gabe. He shook
his head sadly. "It was different in the war," he said. "It was
more . . . impersonal. But this . . ."

"This is war, too," Gabe said flatly. "And probably for a
better reason than that bigger war. You're fighting for what's
yours. Against men who deserve to die. A man who will not
fight for what he believes is right does not deserve to have
anything at all."

"A hard way to think," Tom said.

"This is a hard land," Gabe replied. He looked off into the
distance, remembering a dying people. "So hard a land that

the deserving ones seldom survive."

He turned his horse and headed for the gap in the ridge. Tom watched him for a moment, watched the way he sat straight in the saddle, apparently completely at ease, as if he had not just ridden through the middle of carnage, of men screaming and dying. As if he had not killed some of those men himself.

Tom felt a chill, found himself staring at the brightly-painted Thunderbird on the back of Gabe's coat. "God help whoever he goes after," he murmured.

CHAPTER ELEVEN

Their progress to town was slow. By the time they arrived, a small crowd had already gathered. A hesitant cheer went up when Tom was spotted. "What's happening?" he asked one of the men in the crowd.

The man laughed. "You're askin' us? Hell, one of Davis's yahoos come aridin' intā town, apantin' and apuffin', yellin' his head off about how you'd shot his friends all to pieces."

Tom's eyes narrowed, scanning the street. "Where is he now?" he asked.

The man laughed again. "Hell, he jus' threw some o' his gear onto his horse, then lit out like his tail was on fire. You sure put the fear o' God into that one, Tom."

The crowd was staring at the wounded men lashed onto the travois. The man who'd been talking to Tom stared, too. "Land o' Goshen," he murmured. Most of these men were farmers. They were not used to seeing the results of a gun-fight. They were unused to looking at freedom's price, face-to-face.

The wounded were taken into the doctor's office. Gabe kept out of the way as much as possible; this was Tom's show. But people noticed him, and they gathered in little knots, pointing him out, whispering excitedly. There was no doubt in anyone's mind who'd put in motion the events that had now culminated in the routing of the railroad's hired guns, or who it was who'd helped one of their own, Tom Olafson, take control of a bad situation.

With the gunmen gone and the locals apparently in charge of their own lives again, confidence grew. The election was held two days after the fight. Men rode in from every corner of the county, many of them armed. There was no possibility of the railroad intimidating voters. Davis's tame sheriff was halfheartedly campaigning, but no one paid him any attention.

Davis himself showed up. "I got to give him points for pure brass," Tom said to Hans and Gabe. The three of them were standing on the town boardwalk, watching voters enter the polling place. Davis stood in the center of the street, glaring all around him. His bearing reeked of frustration. Gabe, standing a little behind Hans and Tom, studied Davis. He was of medium height, portly, with a small pencil-line moustache. He was dressed in a dark suit and vest. A heavy gold watch chain stretched across the considerable expanse of the vest. He wore a soft felt hat with a wide brim.

Davis saw the three of them, came walking over, his stride brisk, aggressive. A typical businessman, Gabe thought, all push and shove. Davis stopped in the street, next to the boardwalk, stood looking up at the three men. "Olafson," he said to Tom, "you're treading on mighty thin ice."

"It's summertime, Davis," Tom replied coldly. "The ice has melted. We're going to have real law and order here again."

Davis snorted. "Really?" He pointed to Gabe. "With a felon standing next to the candidate for sheriff? A man with a price on his head?"

Tom shook his head. "Sheriff Smith asked the judge to withdraw the warrant."

"Of course," Davis shot back disgustedly. "Under pressure."

"The pressure of wanting to win an election," Tom retorted. "No one is too likely to vote for the man who let your hired killers terrorize the area. He needs all the points he can get."

"Not that Smith has a chance of winning the election," Hans put in. "We're tired of what you've been doing to us, Davis. Tired of your bullying railroad."

Davis's gaze moved to Hans. He did not reply. Gabe had been studying Davis's eyes. They were small, cold, and hard.

Nothing in there but greed and anger. Now Davis, as if he had felt Gabe's scrutiny, looked straight at him. Hatred blossomed inside Davis's eyes, to join the greed already there, hatred fueled by a simmering anger, the rage of a man who could not stand to be bested. "Some day, mister," Davis said icily, then turned on his heel and walked away.

Hans sighed with relief. "I'm glad that's over."

"If it is," Gabe replied. "I suspect that Davis is a man who does not give up gracefully."

"You think we'll have more trouble with him?" Tom asked.

Gabe shrugged. "Perhaps. That depends on you. All of you here. If you remain strong and united, it'll be harder for Davis to hurt you."

He turned to Hans. "Have you thought about the lawsuit?"

"What lawsuit?" Tom asked.

Hans smiled. "Gabe told me he has a grandfather back East who's a lawyer. That he learned a little about the law, talking to his grandfather, reading his books. Gabe says that we, all of us who have land here, should sue the railroad and demand that they fulfill their original promises about our property rights."

Tom snorted. "Sue? The railroad would just tie us up in the courts. It's the kind of lawsuit that might never end."

"But don't you see?" Hans replied gleefully. "The railroad would also be tied up in the courts. While the suit is going on, they could not just take our land. And, someday, perhaps we'll win that suit."

Tom nodded, smiled. He turned toward Gabe. "You really go after 'em, don't you? From every direction." The smile remained on Tom's face. "By God, for the first time, I believe we just might win."

Then the smile faded a little. "If I win the election first."

As it turned out, Tom took almost all the votes for sheriff. Some of the town wags tried to figure out who might have voted for Smith. "His mother?" one asked.

"Naw . . . he ain't got a mother."

Other county offices were filled with new faces, men friendly to the farmers. The circuit judge had never been Davis's man, so it now looked like the trouble was over for good. If

Davis tried to start any trouble, he'd be on the wrong side of the law.

Within days, life had returned to a peaceful normalcy. Far too normal for Gabe. Time was passing remorselessly, quiet day after quiet day. Boredom began to move in on him. True, he had Naomi; they still stole away from time to time to her little glade. But now that the need for a warrior was over, he was aware of a change in the attitude of Hans and Eva. Each time they looked at him and Naomi, their eyes warned, pleaded, "Permanence. Make it permanent. This is our granddaughter."

Gabe began to look down the road, in the direction he'd been riding when all this had begun. Naomi immediately noticed. "You're going to leave, aren't you?" she asked abruptly one warm afternoon, while they were lying on a blanket in the glade. "You're going to ride on."

Gabe looked over at her. How pleasant she was to look at. A lovely girl. But their relationship, Hans and Eva's expectations, were beginning to hang around Gabe's neck like an enormously heavy chain. "Yes," he finally replied. "Perhaps for a little while. I've heard of some beautiful country about a hundred miles further along. I'd like to see it, spend a little time there. Then . . ."

"Then," Naomi finished for him, "you'll hear about some more lovely country, another hundred miles further along. And you'll want to see that, too."

He looked straight at her. "Perhaps."

He was wondering if she would begin to cry, if she would wail and weep and beg him to stay. To his intense relief, she did not. A white line formed around her mouth as she clamped her lips tightly together, but when she finally looked up at him, she was smiling, even if her eyes were a little misty. "If you were the kind of man I could rope that easily," she finally said, "you wouldn't be you. And it's you, Gabe Conrad, who I've loved being with."

She gave a little shudder. "And the other one, too. The scary one. Long Rider. I've been a lucky girl. Two men all rolled into one."

They said good-bye, then, in the form of passionate love-making. And afterward when they lay side by side, they both knew they were satisfied. That they would miss one another, but that it was now complete.

Gabe rode away the next morning, all his gear packed onto his horse. The three Karstedts saw him off, Hans and Eva standing on their porch, Naomi next to his stirrup leathers, with her hand on his leg.

"Don't forget us," Hans called out.

"I won't," Gabe promised. He touched Naomi lightly on the top of her head, then turned his horse and rode out of the yard. Hans and his two women watched him until he'd disappeared behind the trees.

"We were very lucky to have met him," Hans said softly.

Eva murmured assent. Naomi said nothing, just stood, looking at the point where Gabe had disappeared. She'd promised herself she'd be strong, but she felt an intense sadness welling up inside her. Damned if she'd break down in front of Hans and Eva. She gave a little strangled sob, then headed straight for her room, to weep in private.

Life remained peaceful. "Pretty quiet job, this sheriff thing," Tom said one day. He was over visiting the Karstedts.

"Let's hope it stays that way," Hans replied. He'd noticed that Tom was coming over pretty often. The sheriff's office was located at the county seat, but Tom had opened a second office in the nearby town. So he could take care of his farm, he said. But he was beginning to spend nearly as much time at the Karstedt place as he did at his own. And most of the time he was visiting, his gaze kept straying toward Naomi. Hans and Eva liked that. "A good steady man," Eva said to Hans one night.

There was an occasional bit of excitement to break the monotony. One day Tom was in his office when a barfly came running in and said there was trouble at the saloon. Some drifter was getting drunk and ugly.

Tom leaned back in his chair. "What kind of hardware is he carrying?" he asked.

"Aww . . . an old Colt Army cap and ball."

Tom got up from his chair. He'd been considering taking the sawed-off scattergun, but it didn't sound as if he'd need it.

He was still a few yards from the saloon when he heard the noise, loud swearing from inside, the crash of a glass breaking. He walked up onto the boardwalk, pushed his way in through the swinging doors. A big, hairy, very dirty man was standing at the bar, bottle in hand. Broken glass lay at his feet. The few patrons inside the saloon had shrunk back against the far walls. The bartender was managing to look annoyed and scared at the same time.

Tom walked toward the stranger, alert, watchful, figuring that the stranger was pretty drunk by the slow and careful way he turned around to face him. The man's eyes lingered on Tom's, then dropped to the badge on his shirt. "Ah, shit," the man said disgustedly. "These goddamn virgin bitches done gone and called the local law."

Tom pointed to the scattered glass at the man's feet. "You been breakin' glasses?" he asked quietly.

The man smirked. "Yeah, tin-badge man. This ol' wolf is agoin' to howl today. Been a month with nothin' to drink 'cept'n water. An' ol' Dave, he don't do so well on water. Needs a little o' the good stuff to scour out his guts."

"Well, Dave, they should be pretty much scoured out by now. What say you pay for whatever you broke, and whatever you drank, then mosey along to someplace where you can sleep it off."

Dave's face twisted into a scowl. "Look, mister. No two-bit sheriff from no two-bit town is gonna tell Dave Dupuy to mosey along. Not lessen he's got the guts to back it up."

Tom had already seen the old Army Colt stuck into the waistband of Dave's ragged, filthy trousers. He had a moment to see that a cap had fallen off one of the cylinder's nipples. No real gunman would ever permit that to happen.

But any man with a gun could be deadly. And this Dave Dupuy was letting his right hand drift dangerously near the butt of that old hog leg, so Tom moved right ahead. He smacked the heel of his left hand against Dave's nose, forcing his head back, then reached around and seized his hair from behind with his right hand. The hair was long and greasy. Tom hated touching it, but it made a fine lever. In conjunction with the hand in Dave's face, Tom twisted Dave's head around. Naturally, where the head went, the body followed. Roaring with anger, Dave was spun right around, until his back was to Tom.

Tom let his right hand drop from Dave's hair, although he kept his left glued to his face. It was an instant's work to pull the pistol from Dave's belt and toss it across the room. A moment later Tom had Dave's right hand up behind his back in a hammerlock. It was easy after that, just frog-marching Dave out of the saloon, across the street, and into the tiny jail. The door of the one cell was open and waiting. Tom shoved Dave inside, and while Dave, who was cursing and howling fit to break a man's ears, was still trying to get his balance, Tom shut the door and locked it.

Dupuy ended up paying a ten-dollar fine, and riding on, full of respect for the county's new sheriff. The incident bolstered Tom's confidence about being able to do his job. The townspeople felt confident, too. Life settled back into its groove, peaceful, quiet.

Then the peace broke. Hans came into town one day, partly to buy supplies, partly to socialize; at times the farm's isolation palled. He visited a few friends, shopped for supplies, had a beer at the saloon, all the while feeling a little guilty that he had not brought Eva and Naomi. Tom would have liked that, for him to bring Naomi into town, but from time to time a man had to get away from women, no matter how much he might love them.

The beer put Hans into a fine frame of mind. He was drinking a second, when he heard the distant whistle of a locomotive. The sound brought back memories to Hans, memories of trains in the Old Country, of boarding one and going into the city, a real city, with parks and libraries and universities. Cities with culture. And terror.

Memories, also, of the immigrant train that had brought him and Eva and Naomi to this new land. The long days of existing on hard wooden benches, growing dirtier and dirtier, with little to eat.

Then, the pressure from Davis's railroad, until the sound of a train whistle reminded one of terror, of impending loss. But that trouble was over now. The lawsuit had been filed and seemed to be going well, although it did promise to drag on

for a long time. Still, a man could feel that all was well with
the world now. Well enough so that one could once again enjoy
the sound of a train whistle, as men were meant to.

Hans decided to go over to the station and watch the train
come in. He tossed off the rest of his beer, then went out into
the street. The station, a very small one, was not far away.
Nothing was very far away in this town. As Hans turned
toward the station, the train was already coming around the
bend, big and black and shiny, belching steam and smoke.
Seeing such a marvel of nineteenth-century science always
filled Hans with awe. What an incredible world they lived
in!

Hans wandered closer to the station. The train was pulling
in, the engine passing the station building. In addition to the
engine, the train was made up of a couple of boxcars, a
passenger car, and what looked like a horsecar. Strange . . .
the passenger car was not the usual rather dowdy one, but a
first-class car. Now who would be riding first-class to a little
burg like this?

The conductor opened the door to the passenger car, descend-
ing the iron steps with the hauteur normal to a conductor. He put
his little wooden step onto the ground, to make it easier for the
passengers to get down.

Not that these particular passengers needed any help. There
were just four of them, four big men, wearing big slouch hats,
and long dusters over what appeared to be good clothing.
But these were not businessmen, that was clear from the
gun belts Hans could see each time their dusters fell open.
And all those rifles they were carrying. Shotguns, too. But
most of all, what made these men different, frighteningly
different, was their hard eyes, the eyes of killers, the eyes of
gunmen, eyes glittering coldly above identical, big, drooping
moustaches.

The four men walked back to the horsecar, to supervise the
unloading of four big, powerful-looking animals. The local
baggage man loaded saddles and other horse gear, and more
arms, onto a hand wagon. The four men stood near their horses
and gear, glancing around at everything they could see, not
with any curiosity, but alertly, warily.

One of them happened to glance toward Hans. For a moment their eyes met. The stranger held Hans's gaze for a few seconds, once again, without any real curiosity, but more as if he were a biologist, observing a bug.

Hans felt a chill run down his spine. He'd seen eyes like that before, eyes that looked upon other men as something to be used or ignored or even destroyed. Yes, he'd seen eyes like that before, big men like that, even to the heavy moustaches. As he turned away, walking unsteadily toward Tom's office, Hans's mind was filled with memories, terrible memories, of big men with cold eyes, men in uniform, with sabers, who had come to his village in the Old Country. Come one terrible day. Men who had killed and raped and wounded. Men who had driven him and many others from their land. Oh God! Not again!

CHAPTER TWELVE

There were six men sitting in Tom's office, worried men: Tom, Hans, and four others. All had been leaders in the fight against Davis. They were discussing the new arrivals in town, the four men Hans had seen get off the train. "I talked to the telegraph operator at the station," one of the men, his name was Jonathan, was saying. "He told me that right after they checked into the hotel, one of them came over to the telegraph office and sent a telegram back East. Guess who to?"

"You tell us, Jonathan," Tom said patiently. Jonathan had a tendency to dramatize things.

"The Pinkerton National Detective Agency."

There was a general intake of breath. "They're Pinkertons, then," Tom said. "That's bad."

"Bad?" Hans asked, puzzled. "Why is it bad? I thought the Pinkertons caught criminals."

"They do," Tom replied. "For money. They catch criminals that bother businessmen. They work for banks, freight lines, and railroads. Especially railroads. They even get free passes on railroads."

"Ah, I see," Hans said. "They work for men like Davis."

"Men like Davis pay well."

"So," Hans continued. "They are just hired guns, like the men Davis sent here before. Didn't he learn anything then? Now we have the law on our side."

Tom shook his head. "It's not like before, Hans. These men, these Pinkertons, are more than the law. They have powerful protectors back East. I'm not talking about the men you saw ride in here. They're just hired hands. I'm talking about the men who run the Pinkerton National Detective Agency, the Pinkertons themselves, old man Pinkerton and his sons. The Pinkertons are the protectors of big business, and ever since the war, when the Republicans came to power, it's been big business running this country."

Jonathan, excited now, cut in. "The Pinkertons don't just catch people who steal from businessmen. When there's a strike, they're called in to break the strike, protect scabs, beat up workingmen, kill the ones who got too much guts to give in."

Hans felt as if he'd been kicked in the stomach. Here it was again, as in the Old Country, the powerful, the establishment, doing as they wished to the common man. In this land of democracy! "I suppose they see us as strikers, then," he said bitterly.

"You don't have to be no striker," Jonathan said. "Why, back a ways, when the U.S. took over New Mexico after the Mexican War, lots of Americans went in there, lookin' for land. Trouble was, those Spanish people had been there for a hell of a long time. Had most of the good land, had title to it from Spanish and Mexican days. And the treaty after the war said those titles would be good. Didn't stop land-grabbers, though. Why, they burned all the old deeds that were stored away in the territorial capital. Said it was an accident. Then, when they moved in on the Spanish to take their land, and the Spanish resisted, they just called in the Pinks. Terrorized those people, the Pinks did, an' if they still resisted, killed a few, to send a message to the others. That's the Pinks for you. It don't pay to mess with 'em."

"Well, I'm gonna mess with 'em," Tom said. He got up from his chair, picked up his hat.

Jonathan looked alarmed. "You be careful, Tom," he said. "There's four of 'em."

"I don't think they're gonna shoot down a sheriff in broad daylight," Tom replied. However, the others could sense the tension in his voice. Hans felt very bad, felt afraid for Tom. He'd looked into the eyes of those men. Tom hadn't.

Nevertheless, Tom left the office, heading for the hotel, where the Pinkertons were staying. He found all four of them sitting quietly in the lobby, smoking cigars. Their eyes tracked him as he entered, eyes that showed no emotion at all.

They'd noticed his badge. "Afternoon, Sheriff," one of them said.

Tom nodded, then sat down opposite the man, without being asked.

"Anything we can do for you, Sheriff?" the same man asked. Tom wondered if he was their leader. Or if they had a leader. They all looked pretty much alike.

"Yes," he replied. "I'd like to ask what the Pinkerton Agency is doing in these parts."

"Just . . . looking around," the same Pinkerton replied.

"Looking for what?"

There was a short silence while the man puffed on his cigar. He sighed, then said, "Heard there was some trouble around here. Trouble for the railroad."

"There was," Tom said flatly. "But the trouble's over now."

The man puffed again, then added, staring to the side, past Tom, "Heard something about an outlaw. Some half-Injun with a funny name. Long Rider. Something like that."

"A man with a name like that was here," Tom replied curtly. "But he was no outlaw. On the contrary, he helped the law."

Now the man looked a little more interested. "You say he *was* here?"

"Yes. He left a couple of weeks ago."

The Pinkerton flicked ash into a cuspidor. "Too bad. That's a man I would have liked to have met."

Tom didn't quite know how to reply. He wanted to say, since Long Rider's not here, then you can ride on. But he did not want to see these men on Gabe's trail. "While you're in this county," he said abruptly, "I want no trouble. I'm the law here. I won't have you taking the law into your own hands. For any reason. Is that clear? Is that understood?"

For the first time, the man smiled. He turned to the other Pinkertons, who smiled with him. "You hear that, boys?" he asked. "The sheriff is asking us if we understand."

One of the others finally spoke. "Yeah, Sheriff. We understand. We understand a hell of a lot."

He laughed. The others laughed with him. Tom stood up, ready to leave. The Pinkerton who'd been doing most of the talking leaned back in his chair, flicked ash from his cigar again. He was looking straight at Tom, no longer smiling. His eyes were hooded. "Speaking about understanding, Sheriff . . . do you understand? Do you really understand?"

Tom returned the look. His initial nervousness was gone, replaced by cold anger. "Yeah," he replied. "Too damned much!"

Then he turned and walked out of the hotel. When he got back to his office, he found the others waiting anxiously.

"Well?" Jonathan asked.

Tom sat down heavily in his chair. He furiously rubbed the side of his head. "It's going to be bad," he finally said. "Really bad."

CHAPTER THIRTEEN

Paul Korder had been a happy man lately, a big change from just a few weeks ago, when every day had been a day of fear. Fear of loss. Paul had one of the best farms in the area. He'd worked hard to build it up into something special. Then the trouble with Davis and the railroad had started, and for a while it had looked as if he was going to lose everything he'd worked for.

Then Gabe Conrad had come along, that strange man who at a distance seemed to be an Indian, or at least a half-breed, until you got close and saw those light gray eyes, the long, sandy-colored hair. Long Rider . . . Gabe Conrad. Whatever you decided to call him. Paul preferred Gabe's American name, but his wife, Ellie, romantic by nature, always referred to him as Long Rider.

Since Long Rider had rid the area of Davis's hired guns, Paul no longer worried about hanging onto his land. Now he could enjoy his fine farmhouse, his big barn, his corrals and sheds, as much as he wanted. They were his to keep.

On this particular night, he lay on his back in his fine big feather bed, hands locked behind his head, looking up at the ceiling. It was a bright moonlit night. He could see that one of the ceiling boards had warped a little. Maybe he'd better replace it.

Ellie lay next to him, lightly snoring. He liked her snoring; it was a sound he was used to, a sound that meant he was at home, in his own bed.

He turned his head, looked over at his wife. Her mouth was slightly open, her face soft with sleep, her long blond hair spilling out over the pillow. A good-looking woman, with blue eyes to highlight that blond hair.

It was a warm night. Ellie's nightgown was not buttoned all the way up. He could see part of the curve of one big soft breast. Paul felt a faint stirring of desire. Maybe he should reach over, caress Ellie awake. She wouldn't mind. She was always ready.

He had already raised his hand when he was distracted by the loud whickering of a horse. It sounded like it had come from the barn. Well, where else would it come from? Unlike many of the other local farmers, Paul kept his horses in the barn, not in a corral. Not out in the weather, where they might fall sick or get stolen.

The noise from the barn was getting louder. Paul recognized the shrill neigh of his favorite horse, a big bay that he usually hitched up to the buggy when he and Ellie went into town.

What the hell was going on? Thieves, wolves, or a mountain lion trying to get into the barn?

Paul swung out of bed, paced across the room, stared out the window. There! Movement near the barn, disappearing into a patch of deep shadow.

Paul was already pulling on his trousers and boots by the time Ellie woke up. "What's happening?" she murmured sleepily.

"Something out by the barn," Paul muttered back. "Might be a puma."

Ellie was already sitting on the edge of the bed, sleepily rubbing her eyes, when Paul took down the big ten-gauge, double-barreled shotgun that hung on pegs near the bed. When she saw him reaching for the gun, Ellie paled. "Paul, don't go out there," she said.

"Got to. Can't take a chance on losing any of the horses."

"But if it's a lion . . ."

"I'll take some buckshot," he replied, opening the shotgun's breech. Brass gleamed faintly in the dim light. Bird shot. He slid out the shells, picked up two double-ought buckshot shells, plonked them into the chambers, clicked the breech shut.

"Paul. . . ." Ellie called out after him. But she didn't try to stop him. She knew that a man had to guard his stock, otherwise, how could he survive in this wild place? Originally, she had not wanted to come way out here to the frontier, she had wanted to stay in the city, back East, near her parents, near everything she knew. But, wherever Paul went, she would go, too. And she had to admit, he'd really made something of their farm.

She watched her husband go out the bedroom door, without a shirt. Moving to the window, she saw him reappear in the farmyard. His flesh showed up white in the moonlight. He was holding the shotgun almost carelessly in his right hand.

Then she saw him halt, stiffen, bring up the gun. "Who the hell's there?" she heard him call out.

Paul had seen movement again, near the barn. And this time he was close enough to tell that it was a man, not a mountain lion or wolves. A tall figure had disappeared around the side of the barn. "Hey you!" Paul shouted, starting forward.

Nothing, no answer. Paul was scared; he wanted to go back to the house. But there was one thing that Long Rider fellow had taught all of them while he was here . . . that if a man wasn't willing to defend his property, he didn't deserve to have it.

He was halfway to the barn, his eyes focused on its far corner, when he saw more movement, this time just inside the barn door. Another man. He heard his favorite bay neigh loudly from inside, and with that sound, Paul's fear changed to anger. "You get the hell out of there!" he shouted, raising the shotgun and pointing it at the door. He cranked back one hammer, wishing now that he'd brought some extra shells. Hell, there were at least two of the bastards.

Suddenly, a spurt of flame came from a completely new direction, from behind the smokehouse. A massive blow struck Paul in the side. He staggered, his finger tightening on the shotgun's trigger. One barrel fired, a deafening roar, nearly tearing the gun from his hands.

Ellie had seen it all from the bedroom window, had seen the tongue of flame blossom from behind the smokehouse, had heard the roar of the shot, seen the brighter flare from the shotgun, and now she saw another spurt of flame, accompanied by a loud report, come from inside the barn doorway.

Paul was going down, spun halfway around by the second shot, the shotgun falling away from him. "Paul!" she screamed, then ran toward the living room and the front door.

Two men stepped from the barn door. Another moved away from the cover of the smokehouse. Despite the warmth of the evening, all three men wore long dark coats. They gathered around Paul's body. One of the men nudged Paul with the toe of his boot. Paul's head lolled slackly. "Dead as a hammer," one of the men murmured.

"Dumb farmer," another said. "Runnin' down on us with that scattergun."

"Looks like we got more trouble," the third man added. The house's screen door had crashed open, and Ellie came running out into the night. She was halfway to where she'd seen Paul go down, when she saw the three men, standing over something lying on the ground. She halted, straining forward, but afraid to move any further.

Then she was sure that the object the men were standing over was her husband, and terror, fear for Paul, fear that he might be dying, drove her forward. "Murderers!" she screamed, running straight at them.

She never saw the fourth man, who stepped out of the shadow of the toolshed, never saw the pistol barrel that crashed down against the back of her head. Ellie fell in mid-stride, hitting the ground like a sack of grain.

One of the men standing over Paul called out, "I hope to hell you didn't kill her. The Old Man don't go along with killin' women."

"Naw . . . just coldcocked the bitch."

He turned Ellie over with his foot. Her head lolled almost as loosely as Paul's. Her nightgown gaped open, revealing white flesh. "Nice pair of tits," the man who'd struck her said. It was uttered as a casual remark, with no lust in it at all. Once again he pushed Ellie with his foot. Her body rocked slackly.

He hoped he was right, that he hadn't killed her. The Old Man would definitely have his head if he'd killed a woman. Killed one needlessly, that is.

He went over to join the other three. "I think she'll be out for quite a while. Now we can get some goddamn work done."

"Yeah," one of the other men said. He turned to the man next to him. "You got the kerosene spread around inside?"

"Yeah," the man said. "All over the straw, the walls, the gear."

The one who'd asked the question nodded. "Good. Time to light 'er up."

Yet he hesitated, standing, looking down at Paul's dead body.

"What's the matter?" one of the other men asked.

The man standing over Paul hesitated for a second more, then spoke with decision. "Got an idea that might teach these dirt-grubbers a stronger lesson."

He waved a man over toward the toolshed. "See if you can find a hammer and some big nails."

One of the men was back in a couple of minutes with a hammer and a fistful of tenpenny nails. It took all four of them to hoist Paul's body high against the smokehouse wall, then nail his arms and legs to the wood. Finally, they stepped back, surveying their work. "Christ on the cross," said the man who'd ordered it done. He had a slight smile on his face. Then he turned to the others. "Touch off the kerosene," he snapped.

One of the men hesitated. "We ain't got the horses out of the stalls yet."

The other man shook his head. "Leave 'em. Let 'em burn. This'll be a lesson those clodhoppers'll never forget."

There were half a dozen men standing near the still-smoking ruins of the barn. They were all facing the smokehouse, where Paul's body still hung, nailed to the wall. He'd been close to the intense heat of the burning barn, close enough to be partially cooked. His face was a dried, shriveled mask.

The smell was terrible. Tom fought back an urge to gag. "We'll have to get him down from there," he said with little enthusiasm. None of the men with him showed any more eagerness than Tom to move toward what was left of their neighbor.

"How's Ellie?" Tom asked, partly to take his mind off Paul.

"The Doc says she's half-crazy. Just keeps sayin' somethin' 'bout some men, tall men, an' mountain lions. Don't make much sense at all. Doc says she has a real bad concussion."

Tom nodded. He already knew all this. Anything to put off what lay ahead. But damn it all, he was the sheriff, he'd been elected for things like this. He stepped forward, toward the smokehouse wall. "Give me a hand," he said curtly. And as the stench from Paul's half-cooked flesh filled his nostrils, once again threatening to make him gag, he felt rage flow through him. A rage that made him not care whether he lived or died. Just so this atrocity was avenged.

Tom found the Pinkertons in the hotel lobby, three of them. He walked in the front door, wondering where the fourth man was. The one he'd talked to before was sitting in the same chair where he'd been sitting that other time, once again smoking a cigar. He saw Tom at once, and when he looked up, his eyes had the same lack of expression as before. "Hello, Sheriff," the man said quietly. "Seein' a lot of you around here. Thinkin' of taking a room?"

Tom looked at the man with utter loathing. He knew he had no real proof that these men had been the ones who'd killed Paul, burned his barn and horses, knocked out his wife. But he was certain in his heart that it was them. Not that he could do anything about it. Not legally.

"You bastards," he said, his voice low, choked.

A slight flicker of . . . something in the other man's eyes. "That's not the way my mother tells it," the Pinkerton said, just as quietly as he'd spoken before.

"Butchers," Tom continued. "Doing that to a man, leaving his wife to wake up and see her husband nailed to a wall, dead, cooked. She'll never be the same again, never get over it. . . ."

"What the hell are you talking about, Sheriff?" the Pinkerton said, with just a little bite to his voice.

Tom tried to calm himself. But he just wanted to kill, to pull his pistol and pump bullets into these three cold-eyed assassins.

"You know," he grated. "You burned out Paul Korder, killed him. You know."

The Pinkerton looked from one of his companions to the other. "I think the sheriff's had a little touch of sun, boys."

"Goddamn you. . . ." Tom started to say.

But the Pinkerton broke in. "No. You listen, Sheriff. We're law-abiding men. Hell, we *are* the law, just as much as you are. And we see laws being broken here, property laws, people squatting on property that doesn't rightly belong to them. You've interfered in the legal process, Sheriff. You've interfered with forces you can't even begin to understand. So you—"

"Shut your goddamn mouth!" Tom shouted. His face was red, his heart pounding with anger. He was not even aware that his right hand had drifted close to the butt of his pistol. "You listen to *me*! I want you three vultures out of this town, out of this county. I want you out within half an hour. If you're not gone by then, by God, I'll get together a posse that'll be happy to make you wish you'd left. Paul Korder was popular around here. He . . ."

Tom was aware that he was saying too many words, that it would have been smarter to get the posse together first. He knew that memories of Paul's brutalized body, of the staring emptiness in Ellie's eyes, were robbing him of reason. But what made him stop talking was the sudden realization of where the fourth Pinkerton was.

Behind him.

Tom tried to turn, clawing for his .45, but he was too late. There was an explosion of light and noise inside his head, a terrible pain, and then . . . darkness.

The fourth Pinkerton stood over Tom's prostrate body, holding the pistol with which he'd clubbed him to the floor. The same pistol that he'd used on Ellie.

He shoved Tom with the toe of his boot. Tom did not move. The man saw that Tom's eyes were half-open. "Well, I'll be danged," he said conversationally, turning toward the other three Pinkertons. "People around these parts sure as hell have soft heads."

CHAPTER FOURTEEN

It was a feeling of unease, of terrible growing dread. With a low cry of alarm, Gabe awoke, then lay sweating on his bedroll, looking around quickly to see if anything near his camp had engendered that terrible feeling, some intruder, some danger. Automatically, his hand drifted toward the pistol that lay ready, next to his bedroll.

Nothing. All was quiet, just the usual night sounds, the rustlings of small animals darting through the grass and bushes, the distant yipping of a coyote.

He lay perfectly still, trying to remember if it was a dream that had awakened him. But all he could remember was that sense of dread, of something very bad happening, or about to happen.

It was nearly dawn. He lay on his bedroll for another half hour, watching the sky slowly lighten. He finally got up, a few minutes before the sun rose. It was a beautiful morning, but still, he could not shake that feeling of dread which had awakened him.

What could possibly bother him here, in this place of peace? A little over a week ago Gabe had ridden into a small valley, in the foothills of a mountain range. The moment he rode in through the valley's entrance, he'd felt a sense of tranquility, of belonging. He had not left the valley since. He'd built himself a small lean-to for protection against the weather, which, for the most part had been beautiful. He'd hunted; the valley was full of game. Meat hung in long strips on racks, drying above a slow fire. Some of the meat he would leave as jerky, some of it he would make into pemmican. He'd found the right berries and herbs for the pemmican, and had spent most of yesterday grinding up dried meat, mixing it with tallow, and the berries and herbs, then packing the rich, sticky pemmican into old bean cans. There was so much food in the valley, just for the taking, that he knew he could stay here for months. If he chose to. Not that he would. Soon enough, wanderlust would move him on.

Shaking his head, trying to shake away the bad feeling, Gabe dressed, which was very easy. As soon as he'd decided to stay in the valley, he'd shed his White Man's clothing and put on a simple breechclout. Already his bare skin was taking on that deep mahogany color that had characterized it when he'd lived with the People.

Perhaps breakfast would put him more at ease. Going over to his saddlebags, Gabe took out a length of line and a fishhook. His camp was right at the edge of a sizable stream, at a point where the water moved slowly and quietly. Further up the valley, the stream was much more turbulent, bubbling through rapids. Gabe never made camp near noisy streams; the sound of the water would keep him from hearing approaching danger. Here, the stream slid by almost soundlessly.

Sitting cross-legged on the bank, Gabe baited his hook with a shred of dried meat, then tossed the hook and line into the water. He had always found fishing a peaceful occupation, but today the bad feeling kept intruding, ruining his concentration, nearly causing him to lose the fish he hooked.

The feeling persisted all through the cooking of the fish, even during the eating of it, keeping Gabe from enjoying his breakfast. Later, he tried to lose himself in cleaning and reloading his guns, but that did not help either.

He tried to focus on the feeling, to understand it, but his mind was a jumble of conflicting thoughts. Why? What was bothering him? Was there a message in the morning's unease? The longer the feeling persisted, the more Gabe was convinced that something was trying to get a warning through to him.

Immediately, he felt more at ease. Among the Oglala, he'd been brought up to look at the world as something alive, full of meaning, often hidden meaning, but still, meaning. On all sides of a man, all around him, signs abounded. If you could interpret them.

However, how could a man read the life moving around him, its mystery, its messages, if he himself was not clear inside, if his *ni* was not clear, open, unclouded?

Ni. What the White Man called the soul, the spirit . . . more or less. To an Oglala, the *ni* was not quite the same as the White Man's soul; it was not an identity or a personality that lay imprisoned inside one's flesh until death released it to join the White Man's God, but rather the *ni* was that part of the world, the universe, that lay, not inside a man, but as an indivisible part of his being, connecting him to the consciousness all around him, the consciousness that lay even within stones. A man's *ni* was that which made him alive; it was his awareness. Almost like a mirror that reflected, without capturing, all that great mystery, the endless happenings that made up the world.

But Gabe's mirror was clouded. He could feel it, could feel how the confusions of his stay among the whites, the war against Davis, his time with Naomi, had dulled the clarity of his *ni*.

Perhaps, then, it was time to clean that mirror inside himself. Time for purification. Time for *inipi*.

In itself, the decision to perform *inipi* gave Gabe immediate relief. Quickly, he began to prepare. First, he took off his single item of clothing, the breechclout, and wandering naked near the stream with the sun pleasantly hot against his skin, he began looking for stones, not just any stones, but stones of the right kind. Within ten minutes he had found a dozen, each about four or five inches thick, stones that would neither explode nor crumble when they grew hot.

Next he began to gather wood, dry wood that would not smoke, but would give off great heat. After he'd gathered enough wood, he laid down kindling, and over the kindling, four good-sized pieces, stacking them so that they pointed east and west. He stacked four more pieces on top of the first four, this time orienting them north and south. The stones he had collected went on top of the wood. Using matches, which was cheating—he should not have used anything from the White Man's world—he set fire to the kindling. He waited until the fire had taken, until it was burning well, until the stones stacked on top of the burning wood began to heat.

Satisfied, he went down to the stream and cut a dozen willow saplings, which he stacked on the ground. Going back to the fire, he checked the stones again. They were doing well, he could feel more and more heat radiating from them.

Now it was time to build the lodge. First, he turned in a slow circle, letting his eyes track over the terrain, unfocused, *feeling* with his eyes as much as seeing, until he had found a spot about which he felt good, a place that felt . . . right.

He walked over to the spot he'd chosen, or rather, as he thought of it, the place that had been chosen for him. Kneeling, he used his knife to dig twelve small but deep holes, evenly spaced around a circle about seven feet in diameter. Next he peeled the bark from the saplings, then stuck the bigger end of each sapling into one of the holes, tamping down the earth until the saplings were firmly held in place. He then dug a shallow pit in the center of the circle.

The next step was to bend the saplings inward, using strips of bark to tie their upper ends together, until he had formed the skeleton of a small dome about four feet high. Satisfied, he scouted the area, collecting several clumps of sage. He spread some of the sage on the ground inside the dome, at the north side, where it would form a comfortable place to sit. Other bundles of sage were stacked loosely near the first bundle, where they would be easy to reach.

Over the past week he'd accumulated a deer skin and an elk skin. Neither skin was very pliable, but they would do. He draped them over the sapling dome as a cover, then added his blankets. Not enough. He added his clothing and his Thunderbird coat and finally the dome was covered. He now had a complete sweat lodge, relatively airtight. Ready for *inipi*.

Gabe checked the stones. They were glowing almost white from the heat. Picking up his knife again, he cut a pair of forked sticks, then used them to carry the stones one by one into the sweat lodge, where he placed them in the central pit. Going back to the fire, he scooped up several glowing coals and deposited them on top of the stones.

Going to where he had stacked his gear, he picked up his canteen, then crawled inside the sweat lodge, pulling a flap of deer hide across the opening after him. It was dark inside, but not completely dark. There was light from the glowing coals and from daylight filtering in through tiny chinks in the outside covering, enough light for him to see what he was doing. While his eyes adjusted to the gloom, Gabe threw some of the sage on top of the coals. It burst into flame, giving off a strong, cleansing, herbal smell.

By now, it was very hot inside the sweat lodge. Gabe could feel heat pricking at his skin. He watched the red glow of the coals slowly die away. When the last of their light had gone, it was possible to see the hot, reddish glow of the stones themselves. Gabe picked up his canteen. He poured a little of the water over his head, then, using a handmade dipper, he sprinkled water over the glowing stones.

The water hissed and crackled against the stones. Steam quickly filled the sweat lodge, and now Gabe was sweating copiously, his skin burning from the intense heat. He poured more water onto the stones. There was a sharp report, like a rifle shot; one of the stones had split into two pieces. More steam hissed into the stifling air.

Sweat poured from Gabe's body, ran down his face, stung his eyes. He could hardly breathe. The steam began to diminish, so Gabe poured water on the stones for the third time. More steam arose, closing around his body like a fiery blanket. Hot, purifying steam.

Gabe began to chant, more sound than words, and as he chanted, he felt his mind opening, clearing. Once more, the fourth and final time, he poured water onto the stones. Enough. It was enough. A feeling of peace, of wholeness, was settling over his body, soaking into his inner being. The dross and dirt, both mental and physical, that had caked his *ni* for far too long, was being washed away. He was becoming whole again, one being, one with that which . . . that which could not be expressed in words. His *ni* was once again taking in energy, life, as easily as a man's body takes in air. Inside, he was cleansed, strong, pure.

As the last of the steam died away, Gabe took his canteen and crawled out into the open, into the clean fresh mountain air. Naked, he ran to the stream and threw himself into its coolness. He lay in the water, unmoving, letting it flow over him, letting it wash away the sweat and smoke.

When the water began to feel too cold, he left the stream and lay in the sun. As his skin dried, he let his mind return to the feeling that had been tormenting him. Now, he understood the meaning of it, as if something, some being, some force, something for which there could be no logical explanation, had actually inserted words into his consciousness.

He must go. He must return to the Karstedts. They needed him.

CHAPTER FIFTEEN

Gabe was still several miles away when he saw the smoke, a tall grayish-black column, rising straight up into a windless sky. Half an hour later he sat his horse on a small knoll, looking at the charred remains of a farm. Everything had been burned, barn, house, outbuildings. He circled the farmyard twice, carefully checking the brush, to make certain that no one was lying in ambush. Then he rode in, with his Winchester in his right hand, cocked and ready.

The carcasses of several dead cows and horses littered the yard. He saw that they'd all been shot. There were no human bodies, in fact, there seemed to be no one at all left at the farm. Perhaps they'd run away. He hoped it had been before the destruction, because he knew these people, a man, his wife, and their two children. Honest people. To have this happen . . .

Obviously, the local land war had heated up again. Gabe felt immediate alarm, thinking of the Karstedts. Sliding his Winchester back into its scabbard, he spurred out of the yard, turning his horse in the direction of Hans's farm.

On the way, he saw another farm that had been attacked, although this time only the barn had been burned. The house, however, looked deserted. It was the Korder place. He remembered Paul Korder, one of the ones who'd had the courage to fight openly against Davis and the railroad. He wondered where Korder and his wife were now.

As Gabe neared the Karstedt place, he felt a growing tension in his guts. Would he find the same burned, abandoned scene? To his relief, when he sighted the farmyard, everything seemed all right. Hans was even in the yard, carrying a bucket toward the barn. But the moment Hans saw Gabe approaching, still visible only as an unidentified horseman against the light of the sun, he dropped the bucket and lunged for a rifle that was leaning against the corral fence. Only when he finally recognized Gabe did he lower the rifle.

Gabe rode into the yard, dismounted. "Gabe!" Hans burst out. "So glad you're here. The things that have been going on. . . ."

"I saw a couple of burned-out places," Gabe replied. Standing next to his horse, he continued holding the reins in his left hand, ready to remount. Hans seemed nervous; his eyes were constantly scanning the woods near the farmyard.

"Davis again?" Gabe asked.

Hans nodded. "Yes. But worse this time. Come into the house. I'll tell you all about it."

Hans picked up his rifle, started toward the house, once again scanning the tree line. Gabe followed, leading his horse by the reins. He tethered the animal to the porch rail, where he'd be near, then slid his Winchester from its saddle scabbard and took it into the house with him.

Eva came out of the kitchen, wiping her hands on her apron. Gabe noticed that she looked much more drawn than the last time he'd seen her. Worried. Frightened. Yet, she managed a bright, welcoming smile.

Hans sat down on one of the living room chairs, his rifle close at hand. He motioned Gabe to sit next to him. Gabe kept expecting Naomi to appear, but she did not. Hans noticed him looking around the house's interior. "Naomi's over at Tom's place, helping take care of him," Hans said. "He got a bad concussion. He was out for hours. He still can't quite think straight."

He sighed. "Well . . . I suppose I should start from the beginning."

Hans told Gabe about the arrival of the Pinkertons, of their raiding and burning, of Tom being pistol-whipped into a concussion. "They do most of their dirty work at night. Nobody sees them do it. Or if they do, they don't live to talk about it."

He told Gabe about Paul Korder, how he'd been nailed, dead, to the side of his own smokehouse. And about another man who'd been killed. And as he talked, Gabe felt a slow anger rising inside him. He'd run across Pinkertons before. Some were remorseless manhunters. He accepted that kind of Pinkerton; the United States did not have regular police forces, and too many rural sheriffs were either corrupt or ineffective, or both. The Pinkertons had brought a great many bad men to justice.

However, there was the other side of the Pinkerton Agency, the side that served the interests of the rich, the oppressors. Pinkertons who broke strikes, dispossessed the poor and helpless. Still, he'd never seen it quite this bad, quite this blatant. Davis must be paying the Agency a great deal of money, and money was what the Pinkerton National Detective Agency understood.

"A couple of families have pulled out," Hans was saying. "Who can blame them?"

He sat chewing his lip for a moment. "But I don't want to leave, Gabe. I want to stay here and fight it out. Eva doesn't, and I suppose she's right."

He looked over at his wife. She looked back at him, and now her face lost a little of its tension, replaced by a look of such fondness for her husband that Gabe felt awed by it. "You know, Hans," she replied gently, "that if you want to stay and fight, I'll stay with you."

"Eva," Hans said, obviously having trouble choosing his words. "It's just that . . . to run again . . ."

She said nothing in reply, simply laid her hand on his arm, which was reply enough. Gabe felt his anger grow larger, anger directed at the Pinkertons, at Davis and his railroad, at any man or group of men who, in their unending greed, persecuted others. "We should be able to come out of this all right," he said. "Even if Tom is hurt, we still have the law on our side."

Hans, holding his wife's hand, smiled at Gabe. "You say 'we.' You've done so much for us already, Gabe, without really having any stake here. We can't ask you to do more. It's our . . ."

Gabe's steady stare caused Hans to fall silent. "I'm sorry," Hans finally said. "I know that, to you, what I just said must sound like an insult."

"Enough's been said," Gabe replied curtly. "The thing to do is to make a plan. . . ."

They heard it together, then, the sound of hooves thundering into the farmyard, the sound of horses being run fast. Both Gabe and Hans leaped up, reached for their rifles. Hans made it out onto the porch first, levering a round into the breech of his rifle. Gabe, a step behind, saw two horsemen come pounding into the yard. He started to raise his rifle, then he saw Hans's body relax. "Hold your fire, Gabe . . . they're friends."

As the two men rode up to the porch, Gabe recognized one of them; he'd been in the fight against Davis's thugs. "Goddamn!" the man said, staring down at Gabe. "You came back!"

Both men dismounted. Hans invited them into the house, but they were already talking, fast, excitedly. "We figure them Pinks are maybe headed this way," one of the men said. Gabe remembered his name as Jonathan.

Hans paled. "Why do you say that?"

Jonathan spat disgustedly. "It was that bigmouthed bartender at the saloon. He was braggin' 'bout how we run off Davis's men. Hell, not that he had any part in it. Anyhow, he mentioned that it was you who started the ball rollin','long with Long Rider, here. Well, two o' them Pinkertons was sittin' back in a corner. Heard it all. I saw 'em look at each other, nod, then get up an' head back toward the hotel. Probably to go get the other two, that's what I figured."

He gestured toward his companion. "So me an' Jim, here, we lit out for our nags, came to warn you. Figured it would take them Pinkertons some time to figure out where you lived."

Jonathan turned toward Gabe. "We remembered what you told us. About keeping up a network of local people, to pass information around."

"A good thing for Hans that you did," Gabe replied. He turned to look at Hans. They were all looking at Hans. Eva had come to the door, was leaning against the door frame, looking at her husband. They could all see the indecision on Hans's face.

"I suppose we should get out of here while we can. . . ." He looked out over the farmyard, at the barn, the stock, the corral. His whole world was here. To leave it to be burned . . .

"There are four of us," Gabe said curtly. "And we're forewarned. I think we can stop them."

Four pairs of eyes, including Eva's, shifted toward Gabe. "You really think so?" Hans asked, hope smoothing out his features. Jonathan and Jim were starting to smile.

They all trust me, Gabe thought. They think I can perform miracles, while what we're facing, if the Pinkertons do show up, is a hard fight. Maybe a losing fight. Yet, if someone did not make a stand now, the killing and burning would simply continue, until the local people finally lost all hope.

"Yes," he finally replied. "We'll ambush them. Like we ambushed Davis's gun hands."

He could see both excitement and conviction growing on the faces of the others. They'd fight. "Come on," he said. "Let's get ready."

He sent Jonathan and Jim to the barn. Hans and Eva would stay in the house. Hans tried to send Eva away, back into the woods. She refused. "I stay where you stay," she said, her voice adamant. No one tried to dissuade her.

Gabe took his horse into the woods behind the farmhouse and left it tied to a tree, fully saddled, ready to ride. Then, taking his Winchester, he stationed himself in the clutter of the farmyard, to one side of the house. He would be a roving scout.

Then the waiting began. Gabe was used to waiting; it did not bother him. When he'd lived among the People, when he'd gone out on horse-stealing raids with the other young men, he'd learned to wait, motionless, for hours if necessary. He remembered the time he'd been lying in the grass, only a few yards from a Crow hunting party, when a rattlesnake had slithered out of a hole in the ground, only a yard from his face.

He was not sure if the snake knew he was there; rattlesnakes had very poor vision. Perhaps it smelled him. Perhaps not. Nevertheless, the snake had remained in front of him for half an hour, partially coiled. Gabe remembered watching its forked tongue flickering in and out of its mouth as the snake tested the air. Perhaps it would strike, perhaps not. But, if he moved, if he made a sound, the Crow hunting party would kill him far more surely than the snake would.

The snake eventually crawled away. The raid had gained Gabe and his friends four Crow horses. Now, today, there would be plenty of waiting, but no prize of horses.

Gabe lay in a patch of brush not far from the farmhouse, watching the terrain. So far, nothing showed. An hour went by. Not too long a time for Gabe, but he could hear movement from inside the barn. Jonathan and Jim were not men used to waiting.

The noises from the barn ceased. Another few minutes went by. Suddenly, Gabe knew someone was nearing the farmyard. Not that he heard or saw anyone, but the regular order of the woods was being disturbed by something, or somebody. Two blackbirds flew into the air from the top of a tree. In another tree, a squirrel scampered to a higher branch, then proceeded to scream insults at something below, in the woods.

For several minutes, nothing new happened. Then Gabe saw stealthy movement inside the tree line. No sight of men yet, which meant that whoever was in those trees was good. Very good.

There! The shadow of a man at the edge of the trees. Another man behind him. Gabe whistled softly, imitating a bird cry. He'd made Hans and Jonathan and Jim listen to him whistle for several minutes, until all three of them promised they'd know it was him when he whistled a warning.

Now three men had appeared at the edge of the woods. Gabe thought he could make out the shadow of a fourth man, further back. Tall men in long dark coats, each carrying a rifle. Tall men with heavy moustaches, and even from where Gabe was lying, he thought he could detect the coldness in their eyes.

Gabe continued to wait, unmoving, looking over the sights of his Winchester, which lay on the ground in front of him.

Just another little while, and all four of the men would be out in the open, approaching the farmhouse. He and Hans and the men in the barn would then have them in a cross fire. It could probably all be ended here, the four Pinkertons finished off.

Then Jim, too tense to control himself, spoiled the ambush. Gabe saw Jim step into the barn doorway, level his rifle, and take aim.

Too soon. The Pinkertons immediately saw him. One of them shouted something unintelligible to the others, spun around, and fired while Jim was still aiming.

Gabe saw Jim go down, hammered back into the barn by the Pinkerton's bullet. Then Gabe opened fire, and Hans from the house. It was a moment before Jonathan, horrified by seeing Jim go down, started shooting from the barn.

The Pinkertons were already fading back into the woods. Almost immediately, a storm of well-aimed fire burst from behind trees, splintering wood on the front of the house, tearing gouges in the barn door. Deadly accurate fire. Gabe rolled to the side. Bullets kicked up dust where he'd been lying an instant before.

Those men were good. Gabe wondered if he and his amateur warriors would be able to stand them off. Hans was not firing very quickly, and with Jim down, the odds were now four to three against them.

Gabe quickly crawled off to his left, hidden in a small depression. In a few seconds he was screened by the house. Then he ran around behind it, still toward his left. As he passed the house's back door, he heard a cry of pain from inside. Hans must have been hit.

Gabe reached the rear of the house, saw a pile of stones a few yards away, to the right of the Pinkertons. He sprinted into the open, ran a few feet, then dived for the rocks. A cry of warning had already come from the trees. A moment later bullets were pinging off the rocks in front of him. Rock fragments stung his skin. He crawled further to his left, rolled behind some bushes, then continued rolling until he was behind a log Hans had been cutting up for firewood. He slid his rifle over the top of the log and fired.

Now the Pinkertons were facing an arc of fire, with the barn to one side, the house in the center, and Gabe on the far side, pouring fire into the woods. Gabe saw movement, a crouching man running from one tree to another. He fired his Winchester several times, sending lead flying into the woods, working the lever as fast as he could. There was a cry of pain, the running man stumbled, then fell behind a screen of bushes. Gabe immediately put more fire into the woods, to make the Pinkertons keep their heads down, to keep them from regrouping.

So far it was a standoff. The Pinkertons were sending out far too accurate a fire for Gabe to rush them. And the Pinkertons were pinned down in the woods, unable to cross the open space of the farmyard, where they'd be cut to pieces.

"Gawd . . . I'm hit!" a voice called out from the woods. The voice was coming from the bushes where the man Gabe had been shooting at had disappeared. "Hit bad," the voice repeated.

In the woods, other voices murmured, too softly for Gabe to pick out the words. He heard a moan from the man who'd been hit . . . if he'd actually been hit, if it was not a trick.

More murmuring. Now Gabe was able to pick up some of the words. "They were waiting for us. . . ."

More movement. Gabe sent a few more shots into the woods, although he could not see anything to shoot at. Then a lot of lead came back his way, forcing his head down. He heard a yelp of fear from the barn. They were shooting at Jonathan, too.

Then, silence . . . until Gabe heard the snort of a horse, perhaps fifty yards away, then the creak of saddle leather, accompanied by a low cry of pain. A moment later, hoofbeats sounded from the other side of the woods, moving away. The Pinkertons were leaving!

Still, it might be a trick. Gabe spent another five minutes behind his log, before finally racing toward an outbuilding not far from the woods. Finally, he darted into the cover of the trees, Winchester ready, eyes tracking from tree to tree, half-expecting a Pinkerton to jump from cover and shoot him down.

But there was no one there. No sign of the Pinkertons, except for a litter of shiny brass cartridge cases, and a big smear of blood on a pile of leaves behind the tree where the moans had been coming from.

Gabe tracked the blood stains through the woods, until he reached open ground, churned up by horse hooves. Tracks led straight away; he could see them running in a straight line for over a hundred yards, until they met the main trail that led toward town.

The Pinkertons were gone. Apparently, with one of their number badly wounded. Would they return? Hard to tell, but first Gabe had to get back to the house and see how things were there.

He stopped by the barn, first calling out to Jonathan not to shoot; it would be stupid to be gunned down by a scared farmer. Jonathan slowly came out into the open, clasping his rifle with shaking hands. His eyes were huge, staring. "Jim," he muttered. "He's dead. . . ."

Gabe had already figured as much. He left Jonathan standing, still staring into space, then he ran toward the house. "Hans! Eva!" he called out.

Eva came out to meet him, holding the rifle. He noticed that her face was flushed, her eyes hard. "Are they gone?" she asked.

"Yes. Where's Hans?"

Eva suddenly slumped. "Inside."

Gabe pushed past her, saw Hans lying on the floor. His head was bloody. Gabe knelt down beside him, saw that a long groove had been cut into his scalp. To his relief, Gabe saw that Hans's eyes were open, and were more or less tracking him. A quick inspection showed that the wound was not deep, but it had apparently stunned Hans.

He was looking straight at Gabe; his eyes were starting to focus a little better. "Gabe," he murmured. "You should have seen Eva. When I got hit, she picked up the rifle and started shooting through the window."

He suddenly looked very worried. "Is she all right?" he asked anxiously.

Eva came into his view, dropped the rifle, knelt next to him. "And you, old man. Are you all right?"

"I don't think he's badly hit," Gabe told her. She sighed with relief, put her arms around her husband, gave him a hug. Hans smiled up at her. Both were obviously immensely relieved that the other was not dead.

Then Hans seemed to remember why he was lying on the floor. "The Pinkertons!" he burst out, trying to sit up.

"Gone," Gabe replied. "One of them was wounded. Probably badly." He hesitated. "Jim is dead."

Hans flinched. Eva looked down at the floor. "This land," Eva murmured. "It will kill us all."

Gabe said nothing. Eva had been quick enough to pick up the rifle when Hans had dropped it. But perhaps she had only been protecting her fallen husband. For whichever reason, she had fought.

Gabe went out to the barn to check on Jim's body, while Eva began washing Hans's wound. Gabe remembered how this had all started for him, with Eva sewing up the gash in Hans's scalp after Davis's gunmen had pistol-whipped him. Hans's head was certainly taking a beating. However, since that first day, the stakes had grown a lot higher.

Jonathan had snapped out of his fugue well enough to help Gabe with Jim's body. The bullet had taken him right in the center of the chest, a snap shot, but deadly accurate. Yes, the Pinkertons were good.

It was late in the day before Jim's body had been put into a wagon, ready to have Jonathan drive the wagon to Jim's farm, where his wife would learn that she was now a widow. Hans was still a little groggy from his bullet graze, but was alert enough to listen to Gabe. "I'm going over to Tom's place," Gabe said.

"What about those men?" Eva asked. "Will they be back?"

"Probably not right away," Gabe replied, hoping he was right. Then he added, grimly, "But I want to make sure that they never come back."

Before he left, he guided Hans and Eva to Naomi's little glade. "Sleep out here tonight," he warned them. "It isn't an easy place to find."

"Hiding in our own woods," Hans grumbled, but Gabe had little doubt he'd stay put. He turned to leave. Hans put his hand on his arm. "Tom is still pretty weak," he said. "He won't be able to help much. He's not strong enough to fight."

"There are other ways he can help," Gabe replied. Then he disappeared into the trees.

CHAPTER SIXTEEN

Gabe stopped for a couple of minutes at the edge of a little hill overlooking Tom's place. It looked quite peaceful below. A slender pillar of smoke rose from the chimney of a small house. Chickens wandered, in their usual jerky fashion, through the yard. Three horses stood in the corral, lazily swatting flies with their tails.

However, when he rode down into the farmyard, he was met by the sight of a rifle barrel poking out through the front door. He smiled. You saw a lot of that around here lately. Despite his amusement, he was careful to keep his hands in plain view as he neared the house. "Gabe!" a voice called out. Naomi's voice.

The front door opened. Naomi pushed past the rifle barrel, came toward him. He was already swinging down from the saddle expecting the girl to rush into his arms. But she took only a few steps, then hesitated, hanging back a little.

Past the rifle barrel, Gabe could see Tom's face. A big wad of white cloth was bound around his head. He was looking at Gabe somewhat tensely.

Gabe walked past Naomi, patting her affectionately on the shoulder. He stopped a couple of feet from the door. "I hear you got hurt," he said to Tom.

Tom's expression relaxed a little. "Yeah. I was dumb enough to let one of 'em get around behind me."

Gabe saw that Tom was sitting in a kitchen chair just inside the doorway. Tom got up as Gabe approached, got up quite slowly, Gabe saw, then swayed a little. Naomi pushed past Gabe, slipped an arm around Tom's shoulders. "You be careful!" she said sternly.

Gabe watched Naomi help Tom into the living room. She guided him down into a big chair, then propped him up with pillows. Tom looked over at Gabe. "Still get dizzy when I stand up," he said. "Doc says it'll pass, but I'm beginning to wonder when."

Gabe said nothing. He was getting a strong impression that he'd walked in on something. Naomi was standing close to Tom's chair, looking ill at ease. My God, Gabe thought, they're lovers. Or if they're not, they soon will be.

Well, why not? He had ridden on, as he had told Naomi he would. She was not the kind of girl to mope and pine away. She was a girl who wanted. And she'd been here, in this house, for quite a while, alone with a wounded man, a man who clearly wanted her. A man who, at least for a little while, depended on her. Gabe could see the justice of it, but all the same, this close to the girl, looking into those big, dark eyes, aware of her body, the way she moved, acutely aware of the reality of what lay beneath her clothing, he felt a pang of loss.

He tore his mind away from Naomi. "I've heard about the trouble," he said to Tom. "I saw some burned farms, then I rode over to Hans's place."

"So," Tom replied. "you know what's been happening."

"Yes." He hesitated. "While I was at Hans's, the Pinkertons attacked. Two men from town . . ."

Naomi instantly turned white as a sheet. "My God!" she cried out. "My grandparents!"

Gabe held up his hand. He wished he could simply go to the girl, take her in his arms. He knew she'd let him, but he knew it would bother Tom. "They're all right," he told her.

He turned back toward Tom. "Two men rode out from town to warn us, Jonathan and Jim. We had time to get ready. One of the Pinkertons was hit, badly, I think."

He hesitated a moment. "Jim was killed. Hans got creased."

Once again Naomi paled, but this time she said nothing. Tom flinched at the mention of Jim's death. "If I could only get my head working again," he said bitterly. "Do what I was elected to do."

"I want to go after them," Gabe said, his voice flat.

Tom shook his head. "They're Pinkertons. They have a kind of protection, Gabe. If you tangle with them, the Pinkerton National Detective Agency will brand you an outlaw, and they'll be believed. They'll go after you until you're dead or in jail, and the law will back them all the way. It's suicide. Plain old suicide."

"I don't want to go after them as Pinkertons," Gabe replied. "I want to go after them as common criminals. And I want to have the backing of the law. I want you to deputize me, Tom."

"Ah!" Tom settled back into his chair. He chuckled. "Well . . . I guess I knew being sheriff would come in handy someday."

He looked up at Naomi. "Over in the dresser there. Top drawer, on the right. There's a couple of extra badges."

Naomi moved straight to the dresser as if she'd been living in Tom's house all her life. A moment's rummaging, and she came toward Tom with a shiny deputy's badge. He motioned her on toward Gabe.

"Okay, Gabe," Tom said. "I'm deputizing you. Around these parts you're the law now, same as me." He said it rather tiredly. Clearly, he was growing dizzy again. Then his voice rose in intensity. "Let those bastards put *that* in their pipes and smoke it!"

Gabe took the badge from Naomi, looked at it. A simple tin star, with the words "Deputy Sheriff" stamped into it. He polished it against his shirtfront, then pinned it on his left shirt pocket. He was turning to leave the room when Tom called out to him, "Wait! Are you leaving already?"

Gabe turned back to face him. "Yes. I want to get after those men before they hurt anybody else. Before they decide to head back toward Hans's place for revenge."

When he saw the stricken look on Naomi's face, he was sorry he had spoken. "Hans and Eva are going to spend the night in . . . that place in the woods," he assured her. "They'll be all right."

He turned, then, and left the room, tired of the feeling of strain between himself and Tom. Getting tangled up with a woman, at least with a white woman, could do that to a man.

Gabe rode into town carefully, Winchester cocked and ready. His eyes restlessly swept every dark doorway, every possible place of ambush. Most of all, he watched the townspeople, alert for nervous, frightened behavior. But everything seemed normal, unhurried.

He rode straight to the sheriff's office. Tom had given him a key. He unlocked the door. Inside, the office was dusty, smelled unused. There wasn't much there, a small desk, a couple of chairs, a rickety file cabinet, a couple of shotguns in wall racks, and two empty jail cells. There was a small back room, with a cot. He did not like the idea of ever sleeping in that room; there was a window in the rear wall that would permit an ambusher to get to within a couple of feet of the cot.

He was relocking the office door when one of the townsmen stopped a few feet away from him. He noticed that the man was staring at the badge on the front of his shirt. "Why . . . it's . . . You our new sheriff?" the man burst out.

"No," Gabe replied. "Deputy. Tom Olafson is still sheriff."

The man was looking at him with more curiosity than was warranted by the sight of the badge alone. "Well," the man said, his voice dripping with morbid curiosity, "if you're the deputy, maybe you know something about that dead man they brought in."

Gabe, who had been about to walk away, looked up, surprised. Had the whole town heard about Jim already? Anyhow, Jonathan was supposed to take the body home, not to town. "What dead man?" he asked sharply.

"Why," the man stammered, a little taken aback by Gabe's cold, alert stare. "One of those strangers, the Pinkertons. Three of 'em rode in here a couple of hours ago, with another one of 'em propped up in his saddle. Bullet in his chest. They took him over to Doc's, but he died a few minutes later."

"Where are they now?" Gabe demanded. "The other three."

"Why . . . they rode on out just a few minutes ago. That's after they left the dead one over at the carpenter shop, told Archie to build him a coffin, then ship him to Chicago. They—"

"Which way did they ride?" Gabe cut in. When the man pointed toward the other end of town, Gabe added, "How were they outfitted? Did it look like they were leaving for good?"

The man, clearly a little rattled, stopped to consider. "Well," he finally said, rubbing his chin, "come to think of it, they weren't carrying much with 'em. Just all those damn guns they tote around. Guess their stuff's still over at the hotel. I . . ."

But Gabe was already moving away, toward his horse. The direction in which the Pinkertons had ridden could, along with other destinations, take them to Hans's farm. Perhaps they were going to take another crack at the people who'd killed one of their own. And with nobody there now except Hans and Eva, they'd be able to do as they wished. Gabe had not expected the Pinkertons to attempt another attack until dark, when Hans and Eva would be safe in Naomi's little glade. But now . . . would Hans and Eva still be at the house?

Gabe rode out of town at a fast trot, thinking hard. The men he was after were not men he could simply ride up to. They were good; they were professional fighters. Three to one, they'd probably kill him easily in an open fight. He would have to use his head. He'd have to use all his skill to surprise them.

First, he would take a chance. He knew that a shortcut lay a little ways ahead, a rough side trail that ran more directly toward Hans's place than the main trail. If he could push down this second trail, he should be able to get ahead of the Pinkertons. If—and there were a lot of ifs—if they actually had left only a few minutes before him. If the Pinkertons did not know about the second trail. Indeed, if they were even headed for the Karstedt ranch.

He came on the opening to the smaller trail a few minutes later. It was half-choked with weeds and brambles. His horse was not eager to leave the relative easy going of the main trail for another route that promised a scratched hide and the chance of stepping in a gopher hole. Gabe had to force the animal through the brambles.

Clearly no one had passed this way for a long time. Which meant the Pinkertons were using the main trail. Now . . . if this trail actually went where he thought it went . . .

The next forty-five minutes were difficult. At a couple of places, Gabe wondered if he'd be able to get through at all. Finally, he reached the point where his trail rejoined the main trail. He quickly studied the ground. It did not look as if anyone had passed by recently. Apparently, the Pinkertons had not yet reached this point. If, indeed, they were anywhere near.

Gabe quickly rode down the main trail. He knew of a good place ahead where a single man could command the entire trail. He reached it a few minutes later. Here, the trail took a sharp jog around a big boulder. Gabe rode a hundred yards behind the boulder, where he staked out his horse in a patch of thickly growing alders. He hesitated before leaving the horse, wondering whether to take the Sharps or the Winchester. The Sharps was a more accurate rifle, and hit a lot harder, but it was also single shot. Against three fast, deadly men, he needed firepower. Also, if his plan worked, the range would be short. He finally decided on the Winchester.

Gabe headed back toward the trail, but before he reached it, he turned off onto a tiny game path. Two minutes of hard climbing brought him out on top of the boulder, thirty feet above the main trail.

Now, nothing to do but wait. And then perhaps die, because he had already decided that he would hail the Pinkertons, tell them they were under arrest, keep it all legal. The Pinkerton Agency must have no excuse to send out more operatives. Of course, if the three Pinkertons chose to fight, they would be below him, at a wide place in the trail, with the nearest cover about thirty yards away. He should be able to get at least two of them in the first exchange of fire. Maybe.

Apparently, he had barely been in time. In less than five minutes he heard the sound of horses coming from further down the trail, intermixed with low-voiced conversation. He could not see the riders yet; about thirty yards from him, a stand of brush grew partway out onto the trail, blocking his view.

Another few seconds and the horsemen would be coming around the edge of the brush. He'd wait until they were right in front of him, then he'd lever a round into the Winchester, followed by an order to surrender to the law. Spending so much time on the rich side of the law, no matter how vicious their activities, the Pinkertons might automatically think twice about fighting, if for no other reason than figuring they could get out of any kind of legal trouble with the Agency's help.

But no one came around the bushes. And now the muted voices Gabe had heard earlier were rising in argument. "I tell ya," one man was saying, "we should wait until nighttime, then fire the house and kill anyone who comes running out."

"And I say it's best to hit 'em now, when they'd never expect it," another man replied.

A snort of anger. "After the way they fought? Hell, we already lost Morgan. Those yahoos can really shoot."

"One of 'em can, that's for sure," the other man replied hotly. "The tall one, the one running around outside. The others couldn't shoot for sour apples. Even then, they were only able to set us up like that because we got overconfident. If we'd have ridden in a little more carefully . . ."

"Yeah, that tall one," a third voice cut in. "Must be the one they call Long Rider."

"Couldn't be. He was supposed to have left."

"Well, then maybe they got another one like him. This ain't as easy a job as they told us it'd be."

There was a short silence. Finally, one of the men asked, "Hey, Hector . . . what the hell you lookin' at?"

"Those tracks. Just noticed 'em. New tracks. They weren't there on the trail ahead of us a few minutes ago. Somebody has to have ridden in off some smaller trail."

"Ah, shit," one of the Pinkertons said disgustedly. "Another goddamned ambush."

Gabe immediately heard the sound of men dismounting. No one would be riding below his boulder now. The Pinkertons had complained about underestimating the local opposition. Now, he'd underestimated the Pinkertons.

His boulder was taking on the properties of a trap, with himself isolated way up in the air, cut off from retreat. Unless he moved fast. He slid backward down the boulder, rolling into scrub and small trees. He'd have to get back to his horse, circle around again, try to head the Pinkertons off some other way.

He had reached the end of the little game track when one of the Pinkertons spotted him. "Hector! The bastard's over here!" Gabe heard a voice sing out from maybe twenty yards away.

Although Gabe could as yet see no one, he immediately threw himself to the side. Just in time. A man stepped out of a patch of brush, rifle leveled, and opened fire on Gabe. A bullet burned close to Gabe's skin, tugging at his shirt. Other bullets whacked into trees just behind him. That damned Pinkerton could work the loading lever of a Winchester as fast as any man Gabe had ever seen. Maybe that's what saved him, his opponent going for rate of fire, rather than a couple of well-aimed shots.

Gabe again threw himself violently to one side, rolling behind some small trees. Unfortunately, his rifle became hung up in the trees and was wrenched from his hand. No time to go back for it. The Pinkerton who'd found him was running toward Gabe's cover.

Gabe quickly crawled further to his left, thankful for soft grass which deadened the sound of his movements. Finally, he could go no further without exposing himself; he'd reached the edge of the little copse of trees, about twenty yards to the left of where he'd disappeared.

The Pinkerton was standing just at the edge of the tree line, to Gabe's right, rifle ready, peering intently into the gloom. Gabe slid his pistol from the holster on his hip, moved out into the open, sighting even as he cocked the hammer.

The movement, and the sound of the pistol cocking, immediately warned the Pinkerton. He spun, but Gabe was positioned directly to his right, knowing how difficult it was for a right-handed man to turn to the right while holding a rifle. It became even more difficult when the muzzle of the Pinkerton's rifle snagged on a whippy little sapling, slowing him for an additional instant.

Gabe forced himself to aim carefully. The range was a good twenty-five yards, a challenging shot with a pistol, but if the Pinkerton got turned all the way around, he'd make short work of Gabe with the Winchester.

The Pinkerton had just turned full-faced toward Gabe, bringing up his rifle, when the hammer of Gabe's pistol smashed down against the primer. The pistol roared, kicked upward. The air was still filled with white smoke from this first shot as Gabe cranked the hammer back again. But there was no need. The Pinkerton was falling, and even at thirty yards, Gabe could see the hole in the front of the man's shirt. Dead center.

Footsteps were pounding nearer. Gabe debated going back for his Winchester, but figured he'd be trapped in the little wood. He faded back into the trees and immediately began to work further to his left, in the general direction of his horse. He stopped for a moment, lying flat on the ground. Two big men broke from cover, then came to a skidding halt close to the man he'd shot. Before they could spot him, Gabe crawled away as noiselessly as possible. Each movement was thought out ahead; he suspected that the Pinkertons were good hunters. And he had only his two pistols and his knife. It was imperative that he reach his horse. And the Sharps.

Five minutes later he found his horse contentedly cropping grass. Gabe immediately slipped the big Sharps from its saddle scabbard. He opened a saddlebag and filled his pockets with a number of the old buffalo gun's huge cartridges, glad now that he'd had it converted to handle metallic cartridges. He debated mounting his horse and riding back to the site of the fight, but thought better of it. Mounted, they'd easily hear him coming.

So he started back on foot, moving as silently as when he'd been heading for his horse. It was several minutes before he became aware of the Pinkertons. Oddly, they were talking again. Perhaps they thought he'd left the area. Or perhaps they'd found his rifle and figured he wasn't all that great a danger.

"There's only two of us now, Hector," one of the Pinkertons was saying. "God, two men lost in a single day. We better get back to town, wire the head office, and ask for reinforcements.

The Agency can put so many men in here, we'll flush out that long-haired bastard in no time at all."

"I don't know," Hector replied. "They sent in four of us. That should have been enough. . . ."

"Sometimes you gotta swallow your pride," the other man insisted. He sounded young. Gabe figured Hector must be in charge. It would look bad if he wired for additional help to put down a bunch of dirt farmers.

Gabe began to inch forward, deciding this might be the time to make the Pinkertons' decision for them. They were being uncharacteristically careless. He might never get another chance like this.

Unfortunately, his slow passage spooked a crow that had landed on a branch only a few feet above him. The crow flew away noisily, as crows tend to do, rattling branches and screeching. The two Pinkertons spun in Gabe's direction, rifles coming into position. Gabe pulled back the Sharps's heavy hammer and fired. The big rifle went off with a thunderous roar, belching a massive cloud of billowy white smoke. However, the Pinkertons had instinctively dived for cover, and the massive bullet succeeded only in cutting down a small tree.

Gabe quickly rolled back into the brush, pursued by Winchester fire. He pulled the hammer back to half cock, flipped open the receiver. The empty shell casing, smoky-colored now, flipped onto the grass. Gabe reached into his pocket, clawed out another shell, slipped it into the breech. He slammed the breech shut, then cranked the hammer back again.

"Jeez!" he heard one of the Pinkertons call out. "He's got another rifle!"

Standoff. The brush and small trees were so thick that Gabe could not see the Pinkertons, nor could they see him. Any advantage the Sharps might give him in range was canceled by the fact that he could not see very far. Fortunately, the Pinkertons were clearly not anxious to move into the thick cover Gabe was firing from. A minute later Gabe heard one of the Pinkertons, he thought it was Hector, call softly, "Let's get the hell out of here!"

There was a rustling of brush, followed by the sound of horses' hooves. Still, Gabe lay quietly for several minutes, listening, alert for a trap. Finally, he worked his way through the trees, moving carefully, until he'd found the place were he'd lost his Winchester. It was not there; they'd taken it. Then he noticed, lying out in the open, the body of the man he'd shot earlier. This time, the Pinkertons had not carried away their dead.

Gabe stepped out of cover for a moment, then faded back into the trees. No one shot at him. It was not a trick, then. They had actually left.

Stepping out into the open again, Gabe headed directly toward the place where he'd left his horse. He'd come back and pick up the dead man. Then he'd head for town as quickly as he could. Above all else, he had to keep the two remaining Pinkertons from wiring for help.

CHAPTER SEVENTEEN

Gabe found the dead Pinkerton's horse a few minutes later, snagged in heavy brush. After freeing the animal, he led it back to the body. The horse snorted and rolled its eyes when its master's bloody, reeking corpse was thrown across its saddle. Gabe struggled with the animal; he was determined to bring the body back, as the body of a criminal caught in the act. He must immediately place the Pinkertons on the wrong side of the law.

Gabe headed back for town, leading the horse with the body. He'd meant to once again shortcut down the smaller trail, but the dead man's horse, already spooked by the smell of death, absolutely refused to enter that narrow, overgrown route. So Gabe had no choice but to head back for town on the main trail, which did not please him at all. It would be easy for the two remaining Pinkertons to ambush him. Worse, perhaps even more dangerous for Gabe, it would permit the Pinkertons, with their head start, to reach town first. And telegraph for help.

Gabe reached town an hour and a half later. He immediately headed for the telegraph office. As Gabe walked in the door, the operator was staring past him at the body draped over the horse tied up outside. "Those men staying at the hotel," Gabe said abruptly. "Have they sent a telegram?"

The telegraph operator jumped, his eyes twitching from the body to Gabe. "Well, ah, no. Nobody's been sendin' telegrams.

The line's down. Been down for a couple of hours."

Gabe felt himself relax a little. Wonderful luck. If he survived the day. "Those men," he asked. "Where are they?"

"You mean them Pinkertons?"

Gabe nodded, although he did not want the town to keep thinking of them as Pinkertons, but as criminals.

"They went over to the saloon," the operator said. "Told me to send somebody for 'em as soon as the line's workin' again."

Gabe nodded, then turned and left the telegraph office. His next stop was the barbershop; the local barber doubled as an undertaker. He turned the dead Pinkerton over to the barber, then headed for the sheriff's office.

Once inside, Gabe sat behind the desk. Rummaging through drawers, he discovered some writing paper and a couple of pens, along with a bottle of rather weak-looking ink. He spent the next fifteen minutes writing a report of the day's events: the attack on the Karstedt farm, the death of Jim, the body brought to town by the Pinkertons right after that fight, and the fight out on the trail. He'd lifted the dead Pinkerton's wallet. Various papers gave his name. He entered it in the report.

Gabe sat for a while, wondering if he should look for local support. He decided against it, decided not to involve the local people, none of whom were fighters, in a battle against agents of the almighty Pinkerton National Detective Agency. He'd go after the Pinkertons on his own . . . as the local law.

Gabe examined the shotguns in the wall racks. One had a very short barrel, a real alley-sweeper, an engine of short-range destruction. He finally chose a double-barreled twelve-gauge with a somewhat longer barrel, a compromise that would hold a pattern of shot over a little longer distance than the sawed-off. He'd much rather have his Winchester, but the Pinkertons had it now. The shotgun would have to do.

After stuffing some shotgun shells into the pockets of his duster, Gabe walked out of the office. He stood for a moment, checking the street both ways. Nothing appeared to have changed. He turned to his right. Several doors down he stopped by a door with a sign above it reading, "Justice of the Peace." When Gabe went inside, a middle-aged man, hearing the door open, came out of a back room. The man's eyes opened a little wider when he saw Gabe, particularly when he saw the star pinned to his shirt, but otherwise, he remained calm. "What can I do for you, ah . . . Deputy?" he asked.

"Three men were killed today," Gabe replied. "I believe two of them are part of the gang that's been raiding, killing, and burning. It's all here, in this report."

He handed the report to the justice of the peace, who accepted it somewhat gingerly. "What do you want me to do with it?" the justice of the peace asked.

"Make sure it stays in the legal system. File it. Do whatever you do with things like that."

Gabe turned to go. "Wait!" the justice of the peace called after him. "Where are you going?"

Gabe stopped at the door. "Over to the saloon. I've been told that there's two more of that gang inside. I'm going to bring them in."

He went out into the street. Now all the legal formalities were over. All that remained was to win . . . or die.

Gabe walked slowly along the boardwalk, the shotgun held loosely in his right hand. There were few people on the street, but those who saw him, those who correctly read the look on his face, quickly got out of the way.

Just short of the saloon, the door of the dry goods store opened, and a moment later a man stepped out onto the board-walk, right in front of Gabe. Gabe halted. The man was Jethro Davis.

It took Davis a moment to notice Gabe. He was humming lightly beneath his breath. Perhaps he had just completed some profitable deal. Davis turned, saw Gabe standing a little more than a yard away, with a shotgun held across the front of his body. Davis's florid face went through a series of expressions: first surprise, then shock, then hatred. And finally . . . fear. "You're . . . you're here," Davis managed to murmur.

"It's like a bad dream, isn't it, Davis?" Gabe replied, his voice flat, cold. "A bad dream for everybody. You didn't seem to learn last time."

"I . . . I . . ."

"More people have been killed, Davis. Farms have been burned. Why, Davis? Why?"

"I, uh . . . nobody detests all this violence more than I do, but . . ."

Davis was sweating, nervously shifting his weight from foot to foot. But already Gabe could see cold calculation beginning to work in the man's small, greedy eyes. Perhaps he was hoping the Pinkertons would show up, that they would gun down his enemy.

"It's been a busy day, Davis," Gabe said. "Two of your killers are dead already. Along with an innocent man. I'm on my way over to the saloon to bring in the others."

For a moment a look of puzzlement crossed Davis's features. Then, as Gabe's duster swung open a little, he finally saw the star pinned to his shirt. "You . . ." he said weakly.

"I may be dead in another few minutes," Gabe continued, his voice almost conversational now. "I think it might be best if I kill you now, right here. Then, no matter how things turn out at the saloon, the cause of all this trouble will be gone."

Davis stared at Gabe in amazement, confused by the odd contrast between Gabe's relaxed tone and the terrible import of the actual words. He can't be serious, Davis thought. Then he looked up from the tin star and found his gaze caught by Gabe's eyes. Eyes looking straight into his own. Eyes without mercy, eyes without any apparent feeling. And he knew that this terrible man standing just a few feet away, holding a shotgun, was seriously considering killing him. Davis started to shake. He was afraid he was going to foul his pants. "Oh, God," he stammered. "You can't do that."

Gabe was aware of the fear blossoming inside Davis, so poorly concealed, and he felt his desire to kill this man intensify. No man deserved killing more than a coward, if only for his own sake. For, how could a coward be allowed to live with the knowledge of his own cowardice?

Gabe raised the muzzle of the shotgun, trained it on Davis's belly. Davis whimpered, and staggered against the side of the building.

"If you have a gun, go for it," Gabe snapped.

"No . . . no," Davis managed to gasp. "I'm unarmed."

"Too bad," Gabe replied, almost sadly. "It's always better to die fighting."

His thumb rose to circle around one of the shotgun's hammers. Then he saw a movement off to one side. He turned his head in that direction. From a building on the far side of the street, a man and a woman were looking at him and Davis through a window. He saw the mixture of fascination and horror on their faces. Gabe looked up and down the street, saw others watching, and then he remembered why he was here, remembered his plan . . . to cast the Pinkertons as criminals and himself as the law. But now, to gun down Davis, unarmed, out in the open street, in plain view, would ruin that plan.

Gabe let his thumb fall away from the shotgun's hammer. Every instinct told him to kill this man, to end his miserable life now, while he had the chance. Never leave an enemy alive. A lesson he'd learned the hard way. But today he was not fighting for himself alone, he was fighting for others, for the farmers. He was fighting to end this thing correctly, to end it once and for all, and to do that, the law would have to be seen meting out real justice.

"I'll come for you later, Davis," Gabe said tersely. Then he brushed past the railroad man, not bothering to look at him again. Davis shrank away, his fear gagging him, hardly able to believe that he was still alive. Just seconds ago, looking into those terrible eyes, he had seen death.

Forcing himself to forget Davis, Gabe walked steadily toward the saloon. There was still a chance that the two Pinkertons would simply surrender, certain they could easily beat any charge. That might be good. If they did surrender, perhaps Davis's part in the violence would come out. Then Davis would be squarely on the wrong side of the law.

On the other hand, it was far more likely that they'd walk away scot-free, and the whole damned thing would start over again.

The saloon had swinging doors. Gabe stepped to one side of the doorway, peered over the top of the doors. It was much dimmer inside than where Gabe stood. He could only make out shadows. There seemed to be two men seated at a table near the back of the room.

One of them looked up; Gabe had showed against the doorway for just a second, shutting out the light. Enough to warn a well-trained man. Time to move. Gabe quickly stepped inside, immediately moving to his left, toward the bar, shotgun held loosely in both hands.

Yes, there they were, the two surviving Pinkertons. They sat together at a small table about thirty feet from the entrance. A quick glance told Gabe that there was no one else in the saloon that looked threatening; just a scattered drunk or two, and the bartender, who stood, frozen, behind the bar.

Both Pinkertons rose smoothly to their feet, hands pushing aside the openings of their long coats, baring the smooth walnut butts of revolvers. Gabe had a chance to see that one of the Pinkertons definitely was younger, probably no more than twenty-two or twenty-three. A good-looking young man. The other Pinkerton was around forty, bigger, beefier, with a face like weathered stone. He was looking straight at Gabe, nothing at all showing on his face. "Who the hell are you, mister?" he asked.

Using the butt of the shotgun, Gabe pushed open his duster, so that the badge showed. "Deputy sheriff," he replied. "I'm here to take you in."

The older Pinkerton slowly smiled. "And what would the charge be . . . Deputy?"

Gabe let half a second pass. "Murder. Arson. Assaulting Tom Olafson, the sheriff. I think that'll do for starters."

Now the younger Pinkerton spoke. "You must be crazy, mister. Don't you know who we are?"

"Shut up, Johnny," the older man snapped.

Johnny spun around. "We cain't just let him take us in, Hector. . . ."

"He's got a scattergun, Johnny. And he won't be able to hold us for long."

"That's not true for your two friends," Gabe cut in. "They're gonna be held forever. They're dead."

Shock showed on Johnny's face, sudden recognition. "It's him!" he burst out. "That's the yahoo who was doin' all that fancy shootin' out at that farm. He's the one killed Morgan!"

Further understanding. "An' he must o' been the one who shot down Vince, when we were out on the trail!"

"Calm down, Johnny," Hector warned. Gabe noticed that the older man's hands were in plain view, but awfully close to the butt of that pistol, showing just inside the line of his coat.

The younger Pinkerton seemed to be losing all control. Gabe wondered if the killing and burning had begun to affect him. The young man glared at Gabe. "You killed two good men, mister!" he shouted. "You gotta pay for that!"

"I killed murderers. Arsonists," Gabe replied coolly. "Men that should have been hanged."

"We're not murderers!" Johnny cried. "We uphold the law! You're the murderer, mister, an' you're gonna die!"

Johnny was already reaching for his pistol. "Johnny!" Hector shouted in warning, but it was too late. Gabe had already cocked the shotgun. As Johnny's pistol cleared leather, the shotgun roared, Gabe firing from the hip. The charge hit Johnny in the stomach, hurled him backward. His pistol went off once, sending a bullet into the floor, almost at his feet.

Now that the shooting had started, Hector had made his decision. A decision to fight. Under cover of the firing between Gabe and Johnny, he slid his pistol from its holster. Even as he was gunning down Johnny, Gabe was aware of how smoothly Hector was moving, of how quickly his pistol was coming up to firing position.

Gabe threw himself to his left, into the shelter of his end of the bar. A moment later a pistol bullet gouged splinters out of the bar top inches from his head. Kneeling, Gabe leaned out from the bar, thrusting the shotgun ahead of him. He caught a glimpse of Hector, running for the far end of the bar. Gabe fired, but too late. Hector had already reached cover.

Crouching, Gabe flipped open the shotgun's breech, clawed out the two expended shells. He was fumbling in his pocket for more shells when he heard a crash from the far end of the bar. Looking up for just an instant, he saw Hector vaulting the bar, landing behind it.

Gabe squatted again, shoving a shell into the shotgun's breech. He could hear footsteps pounding his way. Hector was running the length of the bar, trying to reach him before he could reload the shotgun. He'd probably make it. He'd reach this end of the bar, lean over, and shoot Gabe from above.

Gabe reached up, slammed the shotgun down on the bar above him. Then he rolled to his right, as silently as he could, finally springing erect, while his left hand swept the pistol off his right hip.

Hector was right in front of him, in profile, pushing aside the shotgun's barrel as he leaned over the bar, pistol in hand. It took him another half-second to become aware of Gabe's new location, to Hector's right.

Hector started to spin toward Gabe. The range was less than a yard; aiming would not be necessary for Gabe. The most important thing was to make sure that Hector had no chance to fire back. Holding down the trigger with his left index finger, Gabe slammed the webbing of his right hand against the hammer, one, two, three, four times. The thunder of gunfire, one shot almost running into the other, shook the entire room. Four heavy bullets plowed into Hector's upper body and neck even as he was still turning. The impact knocked him sideways, against a shelf of glasses. He fell slowly, in a rain of broken crystal, while his pistol thudded loudly onto the floor.

Gabe leaned over the bar. Hector's sightless, staring eyes told him that the man was dead. He instinctively spun around, checking his back. No one there, just a single drunk cowering beneath a table.

Then he heard a sound from further back in the room. A groan. It seemed to be coming from where he'd last seen the younger Pinkerton.

Gabe shoved his pistol back into its hip holster, then reached beneath his duster and produced the fully loaded pistol from the shoulder holster. Carefully, he moved to the back of the room. He could see Johnny now, lying on his back next to an overturned table. Gabe moved in from the side. Johnny's pistol lay several feet away. Nevertheless, Gabe was careful as he knelt beside the young Pinkerton. He patted beneath Johnny's arms, looking for a hide-out gun, but he was careful not to touch the wet red mess where Johnny's stomach used to be. Amazing that he was still alive.

Johnny slowly opened his eyes. For a moment, he seemed to be having trouble focusing. Then he saw Gabe, bending over him. "You killed me," he said, almost in wonder.

"You aren't dead yet," Gabe told the boy.

As if in refutation, Johnny's fingers scrabbled at the horrible mess of his wound. "Get me a priest. I want a priest," he whispered.

"A doctor first. . . ."

"No!" Almost a shriek. "A priest!"

Gabe turned. The bartender's head was just now poking up above the top of the bar. Gabe had a fragmented memory of the bartender trying to climb in with his glasses while Hector had been racing down the inside of the bar. "You!" Gabe snapped.

"Huh?" the bartender whimpered.

"Is there a priest in town?"

"Uh, yeah. . . . Father Murphy."

"Get him."

"Well, I . . ."

Gabe, who had turned to look down at Johnny, now turned again, slowly. His eyes pinned the bartender's. "You go get that priest," Gabe said, his voice low but hard. "And if you're not back here with him within five minutes, I'll come and find out why."

"Yessir," the bartender muttered. He had to pass Hector's body to get out from behind the bar. Gabe saw him shrink away. Gabe remained kneeling next to Johnny. Wounded, probably dying, the boy looked curiously innocent. Hard to believe that he was one of the men who'd been burning farms, killing farmers, even nailing a man to his own smokehouse.

But he had been.

Johnny, sensing movement, reached out with his right hand. Gabe took it in his left. The blood on Johnny's hand was wet, sticky. "They didn't tell me it was gonna be like this," he said, looking straight at Gabe. "Always wanted to be a Pinkerton. An operative. . . ."

The saloon's swinging doors crashed open. An overweight man in a black cassock was pushing in through the door-way. Gabe caught sight of the bartender's frightened face just beyond. The priest—his flushed face with the sunburst of broken veins in the nose cried out Murphy—cast one glance at Hector's body behind the bar, past all help, then he came striding purposefully toward Gabe and Johnny. "God help us," he murmured as he caught sight of the young man's ruined stomach.

Gabe stood up, moved aside. The priest glared at him a moment, then knelt next to the dying boy. Gabe moved away, until he could no longer hear the low voices of the priest and Johnny, interwoven in careful ritual.

He sat at a table, temporarily drained. Victory, but no victory. Once again, temporary peace had come to this land. This once-promised, once-stolen land. But in the bringing of that peace, four operatives of the Pinkerton National Detective Agency had been killed. No point in bringing up all the killing those four men had engaged in. The Agency was the kind of organization that would want revenge, that would want it not only from Gabe, but from the town, too. Unless enough of a legal stink could be made about what had happened here. . . .

Whistling in the dark. What did the rich and powerful in such a corrupt society care about the law? Nothing, really, had been solved. Nothing. . . .

Gabe was pulled from his dark thoughts by the voice of the priest, who was calling to him. Gabe stood up, came over to where Johnny lay. The priest put his hand on Gabe's sleeve. "He has something he wants to say to you," the priest said solemnly.

Gabe looked into the priest's slightly bloodshot eyes. Honest eyes. Nothing he could read there. He looked away, knelt next to Johnny. "What is it?" he asked, because he did not think the boy had yet seen him; he was staring at what appeared to be empty space, as if into a great distance.

Johnny's eyes turned, locked onto Gabe's. "What . . . what you said before," he finally murmured, his voice weak and thready. "About the killing and the burning. You were right. We did that. Hated it. I hated it. But I did it because the others, they thought it was all right. That we were doing the right thing. But I . . . well, I talked to Father Murphy. Some of the things we said were secrets, and they're protected. But he thinks I should tell the whole world about some of the things me an' the others did. The actual killings. The murders. 'Cause that's what they were. I wanna see all that written down. I want to know, before I die, that the men who wanted these things done, are gonna have to live with them, face them, see 'em in black and white."

Gabe nodded, then looked up at the priest, who nodded back. In his present condition, Johnny could not, of course, write. But Father Murphy, producing a pad and a pencil from some secret recess of his cassock, wrote down everything that Johnny said over the next ten minutes. The bartender was forced to listen, so that he could bear witness later, along with two men who'd been pulled in off the street.

Just before he died, lying on dirty sawdust littering a barroom floor, Johnny summoned up the strength to sign his last testament. By the time the witnesses had signed it too, the young Pinkerton was dead.

Father Murphy came over to Gabe, handed him the pad. Blood had spattered onto some of the sheets. "Take this," the priest said, his eyes not particularly friendly. "And for God's sake, use it to stop this endless killing."

CHAPTER EIGHTEEN

More than the smell, even more than the noise, it was the sense of crowding that bothered Gabe. Chicago. Given a choice, the last place he'd want to be. He was offended by the bustle of the place, a hungry, pushy, desperate bustle, as if the inhabitants were thinking, "If I don't get all I can today, if I don't squeeze all possibilities dry, I may never have another chance."

Gabe had left his hotel a few minutes before. Now he was threading his way along a crowded sidewalk, dodging from time to time whenever a passing wagon or carriage showered the boardwalk with some of the street slush—a noxious mixture of mud, garbage, and horse droppings, liquefied by horse urine and the discarded contents of the night before's slop jars. It stank.

Gabe slipped into a small restaurant, driven not so much by hunger as by a need to leave the madness of the street. He sat at a table. Three waiters were standing near the back of the room. They noticed him, but none of them made a move in his direction. Perhaps he did not look prosperous enough. He was wearing his slouch hat, cleaned up a little now, his duster, and his moccasins. Obviously not a man of the city. He'd left one of his pistols in his room, the one he wore on his hip. Along with the rifles. At the moment, his only armament was the pistol in the shoulder holster beneath his right arm and the knife next to it. He had not wanted to attract too much attention, wearing a pistol openly. However, among these city dwellers, he was attracting attention anyway.

One of the waiters finally decided to come over. Perhaps he was hoping Gabe was a rich, eccentrically-dressed Western miner, who would tip him in gold nuggets. When the waiter reached Gabe's table, he rather peremptorily said, "Yes?"

Gabe let his gaze, Lakota-style, rest on the tabletop. When Gabe failed to meet the other man's haughty glare, the waiter felt contempt, unaware that among the Lakota it was considered rude to stare straight into another person's eyes. Rude and challenging.

Speaking quietly, Gabe ordered coffee, eggs, fried potatoes, and bacon. He'd considered ordering only coffee and a piece of bread. On the one hand, it was probably a little foolish to eat so much before a confrontation, one that might turn into a fight, but on the other hand, if this was going to be his last meal, he might as well make it a good one.

A few minutes later the waiter started plunking down plates on Gabe's table with a notable lack of care. Some of Gabe's coffee slopped out of its cup. Annoyed, Gabe looked up, straight into the waiter's eyes. Finally faced with Gabe's unwavering gaze, that cold, expressionless gaze that told him that this big stranger would just as soon kill him as ignore him, the waiter gave a little jump, nearly dropping a plate of bread. The contempt he'd felt before, the contempt of a city dweller for a hick, contempt for a man who seemed unable to meet a real man's eyes, immediately fell away, replaced by a deep chill.

The waiter backed away a step. "Uh . . ." he muttered. "Anything else, sir?"

"No, nothing. Maybe some more coffee later."

Gabe finally broke eye contact, turning his gaze onto the mounds of food before him. The waiter, freed from those cold gray eyes, felt relieved. He turned and walked away quickly, wondering if he would be able to talk one of the other waiters into dealing with his customer. Probably not much of a tip there, anyway.

Although the waiter was unaware of it, Gabe had plenty of money. He'd had money ever since he'd looked up his Boston grandfather, years before. The old man, who'd thought he'd left no descendants, who'd thought his daughter and her husband had died out on the savage Western prairie twenty years earlier, had been overjoyed to discover that he had a grandson after all.

Thomas Reid was not rich, in the sense of some of the robber barons, but he was well-off. He'd come from a family with money, and he'd added to the family fortune via his law practice. First he'd tried to get Gabe to stay with him in Boston. But Gabe had been insistent on leaving; he was on his way to hunt down Captain Stanley Price, the man who'd killed his mother and his Oglala wife. Nor could he ever have been able to live in Boston. Or any other city.

His grandfather had pressed on him, finally overcoming Gabe's objections, a generous bank account, a kind of advance inheritance. So, despite the waiter's judgment of Gabe as a penniless bum from the West, Gabe had all the money he'd ever need. Not that he used very much of it. Money held little allure for him.

As he ate, Gabe smiled, remembering his grandfather. He'd just come from Boston, where he'd spent several days collecting advice from the old man. Now he was ready to act on that advice.

Finishing his meal, Gabe paid, leaving a normal tip, much to the waiter's delight. Then he walked out onto the sidewalk again. He turned right and walked another two blocks. Once again he halted, checking to make certain he had the building he wanted. Yes, there was a sign indicating that the offices of the Pinkerton National Detective Agency were in this building.

Gabe stepped into the doorway. A flight of stairs lay ahead of him. He slid a hand into his coat pocket, checking to make certain that the papers he'd brought with him were still there. He wondered how effective they were going to be, if they would even keep him alive. Because he was on his way to beard the lion in his den, and the man who ran the Pinkerton National Detective Agency had no reason to love Gabe Conrad.

He'd done some research on the Pinkerton National Detective Agency. He knew that its founder, old Allan Pinkerton, no longer ran it; he'd had a massive stroke a few years before, and now lived, a vegetable, on his country estate. How fleeting power was.

Gabe started up the stairs. It was not difficult to tell when he'd reached the right doorway; a sign was posted over the door, showing a huge eye, and beneath it, the logo, "We Never Sleep." Gabe started to knock on the door, then decided not to. He simply opened the door and walked inside.

He found himself in what looked like a waiting room. Another door lay on the far side of the room. A bewhiskered man sitting at a desk looked up sharply when Gabe entered. "Yes?" he queried.

"I'm here to see William Pinkerton," Gabe replied.

A look of appraisal from the man behind the desk. "Do you have an appointment?" he asked. He seemed to be some kind of clerk or office manager.

"No. But he'll see me."

The man rested his chin on his hand. His expression was thoughtful. "He will, will he?" he asked. "Perhaps if you told me your name. . . ."

"Rider," Gabe said quietly.

The man hesitated. "Rider? Just Rider?"

A slight smile tugged at Gabe's lips. "He might know me better as Long Rider."

For just a moment the man's mouth fell open. He quickly closed it. "I'll tell him you're here," he said, getting to his feet and heading for the inner door.

Gabe watched the man disappear through the doorway. It closed after him. He could hear the muted sound of voices coming from within, then a short, sharp oath. A moment later the clerk came out of the inner office. "Mr. Pinkerton will see you now," he said, his manner wary.

Gabe nodded, then stepped through the doorway. He walked into a large office, literally packed with furniture, bric-a-brac, momentos, and shelf upon shelf of documents. A large picture of a man with a bushy beard and hawk-like eyes dominated one wall. Gabe recognized it as a picture of the Old Man himself, Allan Pinkerton, the man who'd founded the agency that bore his name.

But most of Gabe's attention was centered on the man who sat behind a large desk, toward his right. A big, beefy man, running to fat, with bulging, choleric eyes, and a huge drooping moustache. William Pinkerton, the Old Man's son, the man who currently ran the Pinkerton National Detective Agency. Big Willie, as some called him. Not usually to his face, unless they knew him quite well.

Pinkerton remained seated behind his desk, looking coldly at Gabe. "You have a lot of nerve coming here," Pinkerton said.

Gabe said nothing. Without waiting to be asked, which he did not think likely anyhow, he sat in a big oak chair across from William Pinkerton.

"If you're who I think you are," Pinkerton continued, "you killed some of my best men. Nobody gets away with that."

"They killed their own share of men," Gabe replied quietly. "They were hunted down by the law. We do have law in our county, you know."

"Yes," Pinkerton snapped. "I heard about you being a deputy, Conrad. And yes, I know who you are. I checked our files. They're the biggest collection of criminal records in the United States, and you're all over them, mister. Your deputy sheriff's badge won't be enough to keep us from coming after you."

Then he smiled. "But we won't have to come after you, will we? You came straight to us."

Pinkerton shot a quick glance at the door. Gabe had little doubt that the man in the outer office was on his way for reinforcements. If they were needed. William Pinkerton, like his father, was no coward. Gabe had heard stories of both men beating armed desperadoes to the ground with those big Pinkerton fists. Looking across the desk, he saw no fear at all in Big Willie's bulging eyes.

Gabe reached into his coat pocket. He saw Pinkerton tense, then reach toward a partially open desk drawer. Pinkerton relaxed when Gabe pulled out a packet of papers and tossed them onto the desk. "Read them," Gabe said. "Then you'll know why I walked in here."

Gabe heard the sound of footsteps coming from the other room. Several men. The doorknob started to turn. "Later,

Banks," Pinkerton called out. Then he reached for the papers.

Gabe watched Pinkerton while he read. By the second page, Big Willie's face was turning a dangerous shade of red. "That's the deposition that one of your agents made," Gabe said. "He made it while he was dying. A deathbed confession. He tells how he and the men with him were ordered to go out West. Ordered to intimidate, to burn, to kill if necessary, all for the purpose of driving some helpless farmers from their land. Land now involved in a legal dispute. The other papers are depositions from local residents, testifying to the methods your men employed. Methods that belong in a jungle, Pinkerton."

After a visible struggle, Pinkerton got himself partially under control. Veins were throbbing at his temples. Gabe was wondering if the man's eyes were actually going to pop from his head. "I don't know how you got this drivel, Conrad," Pinkerton managed to grate out. "But that's all it is . . . drivel. Opinion. As for those men, they were murdered, and, by God, you're going to pay for that, mister. You'll wish—"

"Do you know a man named Jacobs?" Gabe cut in. "Alexander Jacobs?"

Pinkerton began to splutter. "That muckraking . . . ? Yes, I know him."

"I've been told that he'd be interested in documents like these," Gabe continued quietly. "That is, if he knew they existed. And if he did know, he'd make sure that a great many other people heard about them, too."

Once again the throbbing veins, the popping eyes. "Why you . . ."

This part had been Gabe's grandfather's plan, the use of the name of a powerful journalist, who also happened to be violently opposed to William Pinkerton. A man who'd love to get his hands on anything that would damage the Pinkerton National Detective Agency. "Not the nicest of men," Gabe's grandfather had told him, "but a powerful and vindictive one."

Pinkerton was slowly getting himself under control. Gabe watched him begin examining the documents more carefully. "These are not the originals," Pinkerton finally muttered.

"Of course not," Gabe replied. He did not like what he was doing. Blackmail. Face-to-face with his enemies, man against man, that was his way. But Pinkerton, with his Agency, was an enemy with many, many heads. Gabe knew that if he continued to fight Pinkerton, he'd eventually go down, no matter how many men he killed. To him, that was an acceptable risk, but that would do little to help the farmers who were fighting Davis and the railroad. Hans, Tom, Naomi. He had to think of them.

"All right, Conrad," Pinkerton finally snarled. "What is it you want?"

"Leave those people out there alone. Let Jethro Davis do his own dirty work."

Pinkerton's jaw muscles bulged as he considered whether he should call Gabe's bluff. He also wondered who was behind this saddle tramp. There had to be somebody. If that bastard Jacobs went after him, using the depositions, it could get messy. Embarrass the Agency. Cost it business. God, but he'd hate to give Jacobs the satisfaction!

"I never heard of anyone called Jethro Davis," he finally said. "Now get out of here, mister, before I change my mind."

Gabe slowly stood up. He seemed about to turn and head for the door, but he hesitated. "Tell me, Pinkerton," he said, his voice reflecting genuine curiosity. "What made the change?"

"If you think your damned lying papers . . ."

"No, Pinkerton . . . that's not what I'm asking. What made the change in your agency? I read a lot about your father, talked to a lot of people. I know that he was thrown out of England because he was a champion of the workingman, a unionist. I know that he started this agency on a shoestring and risked his life going after some pretty bad men. I read all about his work on the Underground Railroad before the war, how he helped slaves escape to the North. I know that he worked for President Lincoln during the war. All I read, Pinkerton, suggested that your father was a decent, honest man. So, what happened? Why did your agency start squeezing the workingman? Why do you smash strikes, drive poor people off land that rich people want? At first I thought it was because you took over. Then I realized that this kind of thing had already started during the last few years your father ran the agency."

Pinkerton started to splutter for a moment, then a somewhat baffled look came over his heavy features. "You're not just baiting me, are you?" he finally burst out. "You really want to know!"

"Yes. I want very much to know how a thing like that could happen."

Pinkerton started to chuckle. "You've got a lot to learn, Conrad. The answer is simple. My father finally got smart. It took him a while, but as he got older, he grew very fond of money. It took him just a little longer to figure out that the big money, really big money, lies with the big companies, with rich men. Not with all those grubbing, sweating little workingmen you were talking about. So he acted accordingly."

Gabe nodded his head slowly. "I thought that might be the reason," he said, his voice sad. "It usually is."

Gabe turned to go. Pinkerton stood up behind his desk. "Conrad," he called after Gabe. "This isn't the end of it. I'll remember you, mister."

Gabe stopped near the door, turned back to face Big William Pinkerton. His eyes locked onto the other man's, and for the first time, Pinkerton felt a worm of fear begin to twist and turn inside his guts. "Make sure that you do, Pinkerton," Gabe replied quietly. Then he walked out the door.

CHAPTER NINETEEN

Gabe came in on the train. Ironically, Davis's train. He was not comfortable coming back to this place, to the scene of his struggle against Jethro Davis, the scene of his brief romance with Naomi. But he had little choice. He'd taken this same train East, leaving his horse and much of his gear behind. Besides, he didn't trust Davis. True, Davis's original gang of gunmen had been wiped out, and now he would get no more help from the Pinkerton Agency. But still, Gabe knew that it had been a mistake to leave the man alive.

He had not told anyone he was on his way, so there was no one to meet him at the station. But the town was small, and he had not made it halfway to the hotel when word was going up and down the street that he'd returned. Gabe had checked into a hotel room, and was washing travel grime from his upper body, when there was a knock on the door. He dried his hands on a towel, picked up a pistol, and went to the door. He slipped the lock and opened the door from the side, standing outside the line of fire in case someone shot through the door the moment they saw the knob start to turn. An old habit.

Tom stood outside in the hallway. "Damn," he said. "What the hell you doing, staying at a hotel? You got friends all over the area."

"Didn't want to put anyone out," Gabe mumbled. If he'd told the whole truth, he would have said that he was only passing through, that he'd had enough of the place, but he knew that would hurt Tom's feelings.

Gabe stood further to the side, motioned Tom into the room. While Tom sat down on one of the room's two chairs, Gabe put on his extra shirt, openly studying Tom. "You look fine," he said. "No more problems with getting dizzy?"

Tom shook his head. "Fit as a fiddle."

"How have things been around here?" Gabe asked, conscious of how stiff his question sounded.

"Fine. Nice and boring, just the way all of us like it."

Tom could no longer control his curiosity. "And what about you? What happened back East?"

Gabe shrugged. "There won't be any more Pinkertons. In fact, I suspect that the word will go out that Jethro Davis is a man to stay away from. A man who brings trouble along with him."

Tom sighed, relaxed into the chair. "At last," he murmured. Then his face brightened, just for a moment, but his voice sounded a little stiff when he said, "Naomi and me . . . we're getting married."

Gabe smiled. A genuine smile, because, while he might miss certain aspects of his relationship with Naomi, particularly the wonderful, exuberant, happy way she made love, he knew that Tom was the right man for her. "That's great!" he said.

Gabe's smile, more than his words, convinced Tom, and he too smiled, a real face-splitter, ear-to-ear, a smile that was both happy and a little self-conscious, because he was fully aware that there had been a great deal more than hand-holding between Gabe and his intended. "The wedding's in a week," he said. "We want to make sure that you come. . . ."

Tom's voice died away, as he became fully conscious of the possible clumsiness of Gabe attending the wedding of his ex-lover. But Tom liked Gabe too much, and was too grateful to him to let that mood last. "Hans and Eva want it to be a big bash, like in the Old Country. That's what they keep talking about, the way they did weddings in the Old Country. And hell, why not? A man don't get married every day."

"And what about Davis?" Gabe asked, changing the subject. "What's he up to lately?"

Tom's smile faded. "That's kinda hard to answer," he finally said. "He isn't his old self. Oh, he's as nasty as ever, but not as slick anymore, not as controlled. Some people think he's kinda flipped his lid. Goes around muttering a lot under his breath. Hates my guts, and from what I hear, hates yours even more. But whenever anyone mentions your name he goes kinda pale and starts shaking all over."

Gabe remembered his last encounter with Davis, the afternoon he'd gunned down the last two Pinkertons. The afternoon he'd come close to killing Davis himself. Yes, the man had plenty of reasons to fear him. He wondered how long that fear would last, how long until Davis started plotting again.

Tom invited Gabe to the restaurant for dinner, where the conversation developed in various directions. The food was passable, but Gabe found he did not have a lot to talk about. Tom was full of plans for the wedding, for the development of the area, full of discussions of his problems as sheriff. Gabe discovered that pretty much everything that Tom talked about passed right over his head. He no longer had an interest in this place, at least, not at all in its daily activities, which, after all, were the humdrum activities of an area full of farmers, of families, of settled people. It was indeed time to ride on.

But he could not leave without a final visit to the Karstedts. He rode out alone the next day; Tom was busy in court with a drunk he'd arrested.

It was a strange feeling to ride up to the Karstedt place without having to check the surroundings for concealed gunmen. Gabe rode into the farmyard feeling naked. There was no one in sight, then a face appeared at the kitchen window. Eva. When she saw him, she let out a glad cry. A moment later she was running across the porch, then into the yard, throwing her arms around him in a delighted embrace the moment he dismounted.

Hans came out onto the porch. "It never fails," he called out. "Leave a woman alone, and you find her in another man's arms."

It was not quite the right thing to say, because a moment later Naomi came out onto the porch, and when she heard her grandfather's words, she blushed deeply, hardly able to look at Gabe.

Gabe smiled, then said to Eva—she was still in his arms, and despite her age, she felt quite good there—"I understand there's going to be a wedding. Tom told me a little about it."

Once again, his smile and his easy manner broke the tension. Everyone smiled back. True, Naomi's smile was a little hesitant, perhaps even a little wistful, now that she had her former lover right in front of her.

Eva took Gabe by the hand, led him into the house, jabbering away about the wonderful wedding she and Hans were going to provide for Naomi and Tom. Coffee was produced, and within a short time everyone appeared to be relaxed. It was another hour before Gabe and Naomi found themselves alone, with Eva and Hans out in the yard, feeding the chickens. Naomi stood in front of Gabe, looking younger than usual, shy, hesitant. "You're not mad at me?" she asked.

"How could I be?" he asked. "I saw a long time ago the way you look at this land. This is your place, and Tom is right for you."

She looked a little perturbed, as if everything was going far too smoothly, as if all the drama was being stolen away from what should be a tremendously dramatic moment. "It wasn't easy for me, you know," she said fiercely. "To choose between you. I wanted you, Gabe. *You.* For yourself. There could never be anyone quite like you. But Tom . . . with him there are other things. . . ."

"I said I understood," Gabe said firmly, and once again Naomi looked confused, as if she were being robbed of something, as if this was not going at all the way she had expected it to go. Easy. Too easy. This incredible man was just melting away in front of her.

"I . . ." she started to say, but Hans and Eva were already coming up the porch stairs. She turned quickly, then walked straight to her room, and was inside, with the door closed behind her, before her grandparents entered the house.

Hans and Eva convinced Gabe to stay for the wedding. They were obviously terribly proud of what they were planning. On his part, Gabe was touched that they so obviously considered him a part of their family. In their happiness, they seemed to have quite forgotten the past relationship between himself and Naomi.

So Gabe decided to stay for another week. But he insisted on staying at the hotel in town. Hans and Eva had enough sense left to realize that it would be clumsy if he were to stay with them . . . and with Naomi. So off to town he went.

He ran across Jethro Davis his second day in town. Gabe was walking down the street, toward the restaurant, when he began to feel uncomfortable. Turning, he saw Davis standing across the street, glaring in his direction. A glare of hatred mixed with fear, a glare bordering on madness.

Gabe stopped, returned the look. Davis continued to stare at him for a moment longer, then spun around and walked quickly down the street, leaving Gabe with a nagging feeling that Davis still had an unpleasant part to play in his life.

It was a day later that Tom came to him with a worried look on his face. "There's a stranger in town," he told Gabe. "Mean-lookin' cuss, carrying a lot of hardware. Gunman if I ever saw one. I'd like to run him out of town, but he hasn't done anything at all out of line. Just sits in the saloon, watching everybody."

He described the man to Gabe, but the description jogged no memories. Gabe caught his first sight of the man late the next day, a couple of hours before dark. It had to be the same person Tom had mentioned, a tall, cadaverous man dressed in clothing that had once been of good quality, but had been allowed to deteriorate. Crossed gun belts held up a pair of Colts. The man came out of a doorway a little ways ahead of Gabe, then turned in Gabe's direction. They passed quite close to one another, close enough for Gabe to notice the cold, murderous blankness in the other man's eyes. Gabe felt a chill run through him. He'd just looked into the eyes of a man who killed for fun.

Gabe was already past the doorway the man had come out of, when he heard the door open again. Turning, he saw Jethro Davis walk out onto the boardwalk. Davis carefully looked each way, like a man with something to hide. He gave a little start when he saw Gabe, then he scuttled off in the opposite direction.

Gabe stopped. Was Davis connected to this stranger, or was it simply a coincidence that they had come out of the same doorway? And if they were connected, was Davis up to something again? Because a man like the one Gabe had passed could only mean trouble.

Gabe did not mention to Tom that he'd made a possible connection between Davis and the stranger. He decided that he'd stop the stranger the next time he saw him and demand that he account for his presence. However, even though he visited the saloon, the restaurant, the barbershop, and the hotel, he did not see the man again. Nor did he see Davis. The stranger seemed to have left town. Perhaps it had only been a coincidence after all, and the man had simply ridden on.

That night, he discovered differently. He was in his room, lying on his bed, thinking that there were only a couple of days left until the wedding, and then he could ride on, when he heard the thud of booted feet in the hallway, followed by a loud pounding on his door. Picking up his pistol, he went to the door. "Gabe!" a voice was calling. Tom's voice. Gabe quickly opened the door. He immediately saw that Hans was standing just behind Tom. Both men looked as if their world had come to an end. "Gabe," Tom blurted. "That stranger, the one I told you about. He's kidnapped Naomi!"

CHAPTER TWENTY

Gabe made Tom and Hans come inside. Both men were far too excited to sit. Tom was pacing back and forth nervously, while Hans stood rooted, his face a ravaged map of shock and misery.

Gabe finally got the story from them. The man Tom had told Gabe about earlier had come to the Karstedt farm, simply appeared in the doorway, gun in hand. He'd made it all sound quite simple; if they gave him trouble, he'd kill them where they stood.

So far, he had not told them why he was there. Hans had wondered if it was a simple robbery—as if he had much to steal. With the man having the drop on them, particularly after looking into his cold, perhaps slightly crazy eyes, resistance did not seem very smart. They had gone along when the man had demanded that Eva tie up Hans. Then it was Naomi's turn to tie up Eva. They'd all expected that now he would tie up Naomi, but instead, he had smiled horribly, run his left hand down the side of Naomi's face, then pulled her toward the door. "This Long Rider character," the man said as he left with Naomi. "Tell him that if he wants the girl in one piece, he's gotta come an' get her."

As Hans told his story, he grew more and more agitated. "I was wrong," he insisted. "I should have fought back before I let myself be tied up."

Gabe shook his head. "He would have killed you. He likes killing. I saw it in his eyes."

"You saw him?" Tom asked.

"Yes. In the street. I think he'd just been talking to Davis."

Rage twisted Tom's normally calm features. "Davis! That slimy little toad. I'll find him, and I'll. . . ."

"I doubt he'd still be in town," Gabe said. "This is a setup. Davis wants us to go after this man, with Naomi as bait. There'll be some kind of trap. And as for Davis, he knows the first thing we'll do is go after him, so he'll be well-protected."

Still, Tom insisted, so they searched the town for Jethro Davis, only to discover that he'd left several hours before. "We'll have to go to Hans's place, then," Tom said. "Follow the kidnapper's tracks."

Gabe shook his head. "At night? No. I think there's a better way. Where does Davis live?"

"Sure! That's it!" Tom replied excitedly. "He must be at his place! We'll go there and make him tell us . . ."

Again Gabe shook his head. "Like I said, he's probably well-protected, and even if we did talk to him, he'd simply deny everything."

"But," Hans burst in angrily, "we have to do something! When I think of Naomi in the hands of that animal . . ."

That particular thought sobered them all. "I'll go," Gabe finally said. "To Davis's place. But alone."

"That's stupid!" Tom snapped. "What could you do alone? Even if you got into the house, you already said that he wouldn't tell you anything. He . . ."

Tom's voice died away as Gabe looked straight at him. It was that same look Tom had seen when they'd fought Davis's gunmen, the same look when Gabe had gone after the Pinkertons. Tom felt a chill run up and down his spine, as Gabe said, his voice curt, "He'll tell me."

It was, as Tom had explained, quite a large house, two stories high, with many rooms. It was situated at the base of some low hills, all by itself; the nearest human habitation was several miles away.

Gabe stood in a patch of brush, hidden by the dark, studying the house through his binoculars. He'd already counted half a dozen guards, spread out through the grounds. Undoubtedly there were some he'd missed. As he'd anticipated, Jethro Davis was well-protected.

Light streamed from a downstairs window. Gabe could just barely make out a man sitting at a table. He thought that it was Davis himself, but could not be certain. If it was Davis, he was probably savoring, in advance, his revenge over his enemies. For it must be simple revenge. The lawsuit was not going well for Davis; he had little chance of stealing the land he'd been after for so long. Gabe doubted that Jethro Davis had been bested very many times in his life, if at all. Gabe had noticed the crazy glint in the railroad man's eyes the last time he'd seen him in town. What Davis was now doing was stupid, from a strategic point of view, with the only reward being the destruction of people who'd already bested him. There would be no appealing to the man's common sense.

The downstairs light dimmed, as if someone had turned down the wick of a lamp. The light passed out of the room it had been in, disappeared for a moment, then reappeared in what must have been a staircase, because the light climbed from a small first floor window to the second floor, then finally lit a larger upstairs window further along.

Probably Davis's bedroom. Gabe had first arrived a little after eleven. It was now past midnight. Perhaps Davis was going to take his anticipation of revenge to bed with him.

Yes, the light dimmed, then went out. Davis must be in bed. It was now time for Gabe to move. Slipping back through the brush, he found the place where he'd left his horse, next to a little stream. He quickly stripped off his coat, shirt, and pistols, keeping only the knife. He took a sheath out of his saddlebags, hung it around his waist, and thrust the knife into the sheath. He wanted nothing on him that might clank, or strike against anything else loudly enough to give him away.

He spent the next few minutes smearing mud from the stream bank onto his face and torso, in stripes of various thickness, to break up natural contours that would give away a human shape. Then he set off for the house.

One thing would help him. Davis, perhaps to show he had plenty of money, had lavishly landscaped the grounds. There were many places were a man could move from cover to cover, right up to the house itself.

Gabe was only about fifty yards from the house when he decided it was time to start concealing himself. He slipped into a stand of ornamental shrubbery, moving through them noiselessly. At the far edge of the bushes, he got down onto his belly and began working his way toward the next patch of bushes. There was a distance of about ten yards of open space to cross between the clumps of shrubbery, but Gabe was an old hand at using even slight terrain irregularities as concealment.

He'd barely made it to the second stand of bushes when a guard came patrolling by. Gabe knew that the guard would be easy to kill, but he would also eventually be missed, then the hunt would be on. He had to get into the house completely unobserved.

Ten minutes later he was beneath a window at the back of the house. Another guard came by, barely ten feet away. Gabe waited until he'd passed, then he quickly straightened up, tested the window, and discovered that it was not locked.

He raised the window carefully, tensing for a squeak, but the house was fairly new, and the window fitted well enough so that it raised noiselessly. One smooth motion, and he was over the sill and into the room beyond.

It was very dark inside. Gabe had listened at the window a moment, and had heard nothing that might indicate that he'd be slipping into a room full of sleeping guards. He quickly lowered the window again, so that the guard outside, on his next pass, would not notice that anything had changed.

Still no sound from inside the room. By now Gabe's eyes were becoming accustomed to the dark. He seemed to be in some kind of storeroom. Well enough. He went to the door, pushed it open a crack. A dimly lit hallway lay on the other side of the door. Hearing nothing, he slipped into the hall and moved along silently in his moccasins.

Navigating from his memories of what he'd seen from outside, Gabe easily found the staircase that led to the second floor. He went up the staircase quickly, putting his weight only on the edges of each step, close to the walls, to avoid squeaks. Again, there were none. Davis had built well.

Down an upstairs hallway. No one in sight. Whoever had organized Davis's security had not been smart enough to put guards inside the house.

He knew when he was outside Davis's bedroom door; he could hear light snoring from inside the room. Gabe tried the knob. It turned easily. He went through the door in one fluid motion, closing it behind him. Instantly, he moved to the side, out of the line of fire, reaching for his knife.

But he had not been heard; the snores continued. A half-moon had just risen. Soft light came in through the window. Gabe could see a big canopied bed, and in that bed, a dark lump.

Moving toward the bed, Gabe hoped that he had chosen the right room, that it was indeed Jethro Davis lying asleep in the bed. He drew his knife, laid it against the sleeping figure's throat, while his left hand went over its mouth.

"Mmmnnppphhh!"

The sleeper jerked awake, started to sit up. "Quiet," Gabe whispered. "Not a sound, or I'll cut your throat."

It was Davis. The railroad man's eyes, still confused with sleep, were staring uncomprehendingly at Gabe. And then full realization that he was being attacked flared in those eyes, surprise, shock, terror. Gabe could feel Davis contracting his muscles, getting ready to shout, or to struggle free.

Gabe pressed the point of the knife up into the soft flesh beneath Davis's chin. "I'll say it once more. Any resistance, and I'll cut your throat, Davis."

Davis froze. His eyes darted left and right, looking for help that was not there. Then his eyes returned to Gabe, and only then did Davis realize who this painted, half-naked savage was, this man sitting on his bed, holding a knife to his throat. Davis froze, and now Gabe could smell the stink of fear.

"Your man took a friend of mine," Gabe said, his voice low but hard. "Naomi Karstedt. I want to know where he took her, and why. I'm going to take my hand away from your mouth.

But I promise you, if you call for help, you'll choke on your own blood."

When Gabe did take his hand away, Davis said nothing, but continued to stare at Gabe as if he could not believe that this terrible apparition was indeed in his bedroom. Perhaps it was only a nightmare.

Gabe pricked with the knife again. A drop of blood, looking black in the faint light, trickled down the side of Davis's neck. "I won't ask you again," Gabe growled. "Who took her?"

Davis licked dry lips. "McCreedy," he finally murmured.

"That's his name?"

"Yes. McCreedy. That's all he ever told me."

"Why? Why did he take her?" Gabe hissed.

Davis swallowed. He could see part of the knife blade. It was a very big knife, and he already knew, from the prick of it against his throat, that it was very sharp. "To . . . to get back at you," he whispered. "You and Olafson."

"How?" Gabe demanded, his voice rising a little. "To kill her?"

Davis started to shake his head, but was afraid to make any move at all, because of the knife. "No. To get you to come after her. To shake the both of you up, so that you'd make mistakes. And then there's McCreedy. He . . . he's heard of you, wants to take you on. He's . . . a little crazy, I think."

Gabe felt a great relief. He'd been afraid that by now Naomi would be dead. But if she was being used principally as a hostage, as bait . . .

"Where is he keeping her?" Gabe snapped.

Davis started to say something, then hesitated. To Gabe's amazement, that cold, calculating light was once again appearing in the other man's eyes. Even with a knife against his throat. "If I tell you," Davis said, "you'll just kill me and leave."

Gabe looked steadily at the other man. True, that plan had crossed his mind. Davis read his silence as confirmation. "There's no point in my telling you a damned thing if you're going to kill me anyhow."

Gabe continued to stare at Davis. "There are ways to die," he finally said. "I can choose one of the more painful ones, then I can follow this McCreedy's tracks in the morning."

"But it's a long time until morning," Davis said quickly. "And no telling what might have happened to the girl by then. Like I said, McCreedy is not quite all there."

"Yeah," Gabe replied softly. "Just the kind of man you'd hire, Davis."

He had to get to the truth, and fast. He'd sensed it all along, the need to get to Naomi before McCreedy . . . No point in thinking about that.

"I'll swear, Davis, that if you tell me the truth, I'll let you live. I'll swear on my honor."

The words came out so reluctantly, with so much obvious pain, that Davis knew Gabe meant them. Davis himself, businessman to the core, had no honor at all, only a capacity for making deals. He'd sensed all along, had always known, that this man, his enemy, was another kind of person, that he had a weakness Davis did not share. Honesty. "Swear!" Davis gritted out.

Gabe nodded. "I swear it. I'll let you live."

The words hurt him. Once again he was going to have to leave this man alive, to threaten his back. Davis smiled, knowing he'd won. He then described a place Gabe had once passed a few weeks before, a narrow cave entrance at the head of a small canyon. "That's where he said he'd take her," Davis said. "I thought it was a stupid plan, but McCreedy said that when you came after her, it would be a perfect place to kill you. You'd never shoot into the cave, knowing the girl was in there with him."

Gabe sensed that Davis was telling the truth. Why not? If Gabe went after Naomi, McCreedy stood a good chance of killing him. Which had undoubtedly been the plan all along.

Davis misread Gabe's silence, his grim stare. "You . . . you promised," he said weakly.

"Yes, I did promise. To leave you alive," Gabe said. With lightning speed, he took the blade away from Davis's throat, then smashed him alongside the head with the knife's heavy butt. Davis groaned, then fell back onto his pillow, unconscious. Gabe quickly stood up. Davis remained still, his breath wheezing in and out as a slight, unhealthy snore. Gabe crept out quickly. He could deal with Davis another day. What mattered most now was getting to Naomi. Before McCreedy . . . But no, he couldn't think about that, mustn't think of it. He must think only of saving Naomi.

CHAPTER TWENTY-ONE

The cave was as Gabe remembered it, a black gash in a sheer stone cliff, the opening narrowing to a point at the top, then widening unevenly as it neared the ground.

The sun had just come up. It was a beautiful morning; Gabe had time to realize the loveliness of the day before his mind returned to the ugly realities he was about to face.

He knew it would be better to approach the place at night, when he might be able to get a lot closer without being seen, and perhaps surprise McCreedy. If he actually was in the cave. But the thought of leaving McCreedy alone with Naomi for an entire day did not appeal to him.

He rode closer, then stopped about a hundred yards away, partially concealed behind an outcrop of rock. He dismounted. "McCreedy!" he called out loudly.

For a while, there was no response. Then he thought he saw movement from just inside the cave entrance. "Who the hell's out there?" a voice replied.

Gabe hesitated. "Long Rider," he finally said.

Laughter floated back at him from the cave mouth. Strange, wild laughter that set his teeth on edge. "I knew you'd come," the voice called out. "Are you alone?"

"Yes."

"Show yourself."

"You first."

More laughter. Then the shadowy movement within the cave mouth resolved into a person, Naomi, being shoved a little ways out into the open, partly obscuring a man standing just behind her. Gabe fastened his attention on the girl. As far as he could tell, she looked unhurt, although her dress was torn at the shoulder.

"This who you're looking for?" the voice called out. Naomi and the man stepped further into the open, and now Gabe could see that it was indeed the cadaverous individual he'd seen in town the day before. McCreedy.

"Let her go," Gabe called out. "Then you and I can settle this between us."

Again, that wild laughter. "That ain't the way I see it, buster. If I let her go, then you can pen me up in here and send the girl for help. Uh-uh. This is gonna be between you and me, all right, but usin' my rules. I heard about you, been hearing the name Long Rider for quite a while. You got a real reputation, mister, and I'm gonna find out if there's anything to it. Now, you just step on out of cover, Mr. Long Rider, and make sure you leave your rifles behind."

Gabe hesitated. If he stepped out into the open, then McCreedy could simply produce a rifle from within the cave and gun him down before he could get within pistol range. As if aware of his doubts, McCreedy poked Naomi in the side. Gabe saw her flinch away in pain, then McCreedy was saying something to her that Gabe could not hear.

Finally, Naomi called out, "He hasn't got a rifle, Gabe."

Now that Naomi had finally spoken, Gabe called to her. "Are you all right? You haven't been . . . hurt?"

It was McCreedy who answered, first with his cackling laughter, then he said, "You mean, have I had the little lady yet? Have I done unspeakable things to her tender young body?"

Again the laughter, even wilder. Gabe's flesh crawled. "Not yet, Mr. Long Rider. I been savin' all that until after I kill you."

He poked Naomi in the ribs again. "Then this little lady is gonna spend a hard couple of hours."

McCreedy reached out, squeezed one of Naomi's breasts. The girl flinched away. Gabe took a quick step forward. "That's right, big man," McCreedy said, sneering. "You come right ahead and save her."

Gabe halted. He was still close enough to the rock outcrop to be able to leap back toward his horse and grab a rifle. But McCreedy was even closer to cover, and besides, he had Naomi. There was nothing to do but head toward the man, and end it, one way or the other, by killing or being killed.

But he could not think of dying. Then Naomi would be at McCreedy's mercy. Gabe continued forward, walking slowly, his eyes fastened on the other man, waiting for any moves that might signal danger.

Once Gabe had walked out into the open, McCreedy did the same. He stopped about six feet in front of the cave entrance, standing spraddle-legged, with his hands caressing the butts of the twin Colts riding low on his hips. Gabe was close enough now to see the excited gleam in the other man's eyes. "I guess you maybe heard of me," McCreedy called out.

"Never," Gabe replied.

He was close enough to see the scowl that crossed over McCreedy's thin features. "Hell, mister, I've killed my share of men, more than my share, and killed 'em clean. You musta heard of me."

They were close enough so that they could talk in normal tones. And still Gabe continued forward. He wanted to be close enough so that he could not miss. He suspected he would have only one chance, and if he failed, not only would he pay with his life, but so would Naomi. He wished now that he'd gone for Tom. But he'd wanted to reach McCreedy and Naomi as quickly as possible. "I don't pay attention to rumors about back shooters," Gabe replied caustically.

Wild anger flared across McCreedy's face. "Back shooter?" he screamed. "I ain't never shot a man in the back in my life! All from the front, right through the heart!"

Gabe smiled. He wanted to get McCreedy as riled as possible, then perhaps he would make a mistake. But when Gabe smiled, McCreedy instantly calmed himself. "You're a dead man, Mr. Long Rider," he hissed. "And you . . . I ain't gonna shoot you through the heart. I'm gonna gut shoot you. Then you can watch while I take the girl apart."

Gabe was close enough now to see the madness in the other man's eyes. A man who liked killing for its own sake, who fed his own ego on the thrill of ending the lives of others. A man with a miserable, shriveled soul.

He stopped about ten yards away from McCreedy. McCreedy stood facing him, still spraddle-legged, but now with his thumbs hooked in his cartridge belts, as if to show that he could afford to give Gabe a little extra chance. And that it would not matter, that he would kill him anyhow.

Naomi was positioned to McCreedy's right, a few yards away, leaning back against the stone cliff, her face white with strain, one hand scrabbling at the crumbling cliff face. Gabe gave her a quick look, then returned his gaze to McCreedy.

So far Gabe had been careful to keep his hands away from the pistol on his hip. He was wearing his Thunderbird coat, and wished he'd left it with his horse, because the heavy leather would slow him down. He carefully brushed the edge of the coat back along his side, baring the butt of his pistol.

"A lefty, huh?" McCreedy said. His voice was thin now, slightly strained, not with fear, but with joyful, almost sexual excitement. Gabe kept his left hand high, with the little finger lightly scratching at his chest, as if he did not have a care in the world, as if he were not about to engage in a life and death struggle.

He sensed it when McCreedy was about to start his draw, saw the sudden tightening of flesh around the other man's eyes. Gabe slipped his left hand beneath the lapel of his coat, reaching for the pistol beneath his right arm, the pistol McCreedy would not know he had. The maneuver gave him a slight shading of advantage, but he was still pulling the pistol free from its holster when he realized that it would not be enough. McCreedy was fast, incredibly fast, perhaps the fastest man with a gun Gabe had ever seen. Gabe was still clearing leather when McCreedy cocked his pistol, leveled it at Gabe. At his belly, just as he'd promised.

But now Naomi was moving. Her scrabblings at the face of the cliff had not been induced by fear. She'd worked a small stone loose, one with sharp edges. Just as McCreedy was getting ready to shoot, she screamed, an inarticulate cry of hatred and anger, and threw the stone at McCreedy.

It was the cry rather than the stone, plus the unexpected movement off to his right, that most affected McCreedy. The stone had not yet reached him when he fired, but by then his aim had been ruined, and the bullet flew just wide of Gabe, plucking at his right sleeve. By then Gabe had cocked his own pistol, and he fired before McCreedy could get off another shot. His bullet, not aimed as well as he would have liked, took McCreedy in the lower chest, just below the sternum. The heavy bullet knocked all the air from McCreedy's lungs and pushed him backward. He still held his pistol, and after a moment's shocked disbelief that he'd been hit, he tried to raise the muzzle to fire at Gabe.

But by now Gabe was walking forward, steadily, purposefully, and with each step he fired his pistol, pumping four more bullets into McCreedy's rail-thin body. Each impact slammed the gunman backward, until he finally collided with the stone cliff. Only then did he go down, sliding slowly down the rock, leaving a smear of blood behind him.

McCreedy turned his head, once, to face Naomi. "You . . ." he tried to say, but the words were stifled by a big bubble of blood that swelled from his mouth.

Gabe walked close, kicked the gun out of McCreedy's hand. When he looked at the man's face again the staring, sightless eyes told him that McCreedy was dead.

Then Naomi was in his arms. "Oh, Gabe," she cried. "I was so afraid he was going to kill you!"

"If it wasn't for you, he would have," Gabe replied somberly. "And you? He really didn't . . . hurt you?"

She stepped back. She was smiling now, through tears. "No," she replied, shaking her head. "He pushed me around a little, and he kind of . . . felt me here and there. But I don't think he really knew how to do more. He was . . . a strange man, Gabe. Sick in the head."

Gabe looked over at the corpse. "Yeah. Let's get the hell out of here."

That suited Naomi fine. Her horse, along with McCreedy's, was inside the cave. Gabe retrieved both animals, who seemed glad to see daylight again. He was considering hoisting McCreedy's body up onto the back of his horse, but Naomi, as if reading his intention, said, "Leave him here. I couldn't stand riding back with him anywhere near me."

So they saddled Naomi's horse and let McCreedy's go. Within minutes they were riding away from the cave, heading toward the main trail back to town. As they rode, Gabe stole a couple of glances in Naomi's direction. She was all the woman he'd thought she was. Instead of just standing there, helpless, watching him go against McCreedy alone, she had taken a hand in the fight, turned the tables in his favor. Any woman with that much spunk deserved to survive.

She caught him looking at her. "I knew you'd come," she said, her voice low. "I knew that it would be you, and not Tom."

"He's half out of his mind with worry," Gabe replied.

She said nothing. Ten minutes passed. Gabe noticed that she was looking around her, at the terrain. Just as they were passing a grassy little glade, she called out, "Pull up, Gabe. Stop."

He pulled his horse to a halt, then looked around quickly, studying the landscape for possible trouble. He saw nothing, and by the time he looked back at Naomi, she had dismounted. She was looking up at him. "Gabe," she said. "Get down."

Was she hurt? Were her nerves finally failing her? He quickly dismounted, went up to her. She moved close, pressed her breasts against his chest, and when he looked down into her eyes, when he saw how huge they appeared, how boundless, he knew what she wanted. Her arms went around him. "Make love to me, Gabe," she murmured.

Automatically, his arms started to encircle the girl's warm body, but he stopped himself. "And . . . Tom?" he asked.

She hesitated a moment. "I still want to marry him, Gabe," she replied, her voice urgent. "But I want this from you. This one last thing. This one last time."

He stepped back a pace. "I can't do that, Naomi. It wouldn't be right. It wouldn't be fair to Tom."

She looked down for a moment, then looked back up, straight into his eyes. "Tom isn't here, Gabe. There's just you and me, and we've been through . . . something terrible together. I need you, Gabe. Need you this one last time. Need you to make me forget that . . . terrible man. The things he said to me. I need you, Gabe. Need this so much."

Still, Gabe hesitated. He knew what was fueling at least part of the girl's desire . . . the immediacy of life and death, the terror of the past twenty-four hours. When death was around, passion blossomed. All kinds of passion.

Those eyes. He felt himself sinking into them, rediscovering the memories of the many times they'd made love. He thought of his own near brush with death, but most of all, it was those eyes.

They made love on the ground, on a little patch of grass, Gabe tearing at Naomi's clothes, wanting to see, touch, experience her body, all of it, once again.

It was over in a very short time, and neither said much as they dressed. The rest of the way back to town, they did not look at each other much, not out of shame or guilt, but because there was nothing more to be said. Or done. They reached town in the afternoon, riding down the main street together. Tom and Hans saw them when they were still fifty yards from the sheriff's office. Both men came running out into the dusty street, their faces ravaged by a combination of worry and joy. "My God!" Hans called out. "Naomi! That man . . . did he . . . ?"

For the first time, Naomi laughed. "Is that all you men can think about?" she asked, just a little tartly. "No, he didn't. Gabe got there in time."

Gabe was aware of the look of relief on Tom's face, and he felt just slightly guilty. Hans and Tom helped Naomi down from her horse, as if she were so fragile she'd break. But if they could have seen her throw that stone . . .

Tom turned toward Gabe. "Davis is in town," he said. "I didn't know what to do, didn't know what you'd already done. I didn't want to wreck anything you'd set up."

"It worked out," Gabe replied. "The man he hired to take Naomi is dead. Now it's Davis's turn. You just tell me where he is."

Tom shook his head. "No," he replied, his voice hard. "Davis is mine."

Tom started to walk away down the street. Gabe dismounted, and followed a few steps behind, but he knew that he would not interfere. It was a surprise, then, when Davis himself stepped out from between two buildings, holding a pistol. He was closer to Tom, but it was Gabe he was looking at, and even from this distance, Gabe could see the mad glitter in the railroad man's eyes. "You!" he screamed at Gabe. "You ruined everything. You made me—"

"You're under arrest, Davis," Tom called out, drawing his own pistol. But Davis paid Tom no attention. Instead, he raised his pistol and aimed it at Gabe.

Tom fired first. His bullet took Davis square in the chest. Davis staggered, then fell flat onto his back in the middle of the street, his pistol spinning away, out of reach. Tom walked up to Davis, prodded him with his foot. "Dead," he said.

No one said anything for a moment, until Hans spoke, his voice low, almost without expression. "Then it is finally over."

The wedding was quite a success, the gala event that Eva had wanted it to be. Naomi, wearing a white dress that had taken Eva days to make, stood before Father Murphy alongside Tom, who was looking very sober in his only suit. The whole town was there, including Gabe, who sat in the front pew with Eva. At one point in the ceremony Naomi looked over her shoulder at Gabe, looked at him steadily for several seconds. It was one of the smuggest looks he had ever seen. Why? Because of the marriage?

Naomi smiled to herself when she saw Gabe's face. If he only knew. Perhaps he thought she was gloating because she had her man now, a man all her own, a man who would be hers for the rest of her life. A man that she knew would make her happy. A man who would make a home for her, a man who would give her many fine children.

Yes, she would have children. She did not know exactly how many she would have from Tom. But . . . from Gabe . . .

Her mind went back to their last lovemaking, along the side of the trail, after the two of them, together, had killed Davis's insane gunman. She remembered the way they had made love, the intensity of it. She would always remember that last time.

Yes, she'd have many babies, many from her husband, a man she truly loved. But the first would be Gabe's. She'd always known he would ride away; in fact, it was planned that he would leave immediately after the wedding. He would ride out of her life forever, following whatever strange dream he was chasing. He would be hers no more.

But, unknowingly, he had left part of himself behind. With her. Part of himself that she would cherish for the rest of her life.

And with a look of quiet triumph, she turned back to the priest. "I do," she said firmly.

SPECIAL PREVIEW!

*At the heart of a great nation
lay the proud spirit of the railroads . . .*

RAILS WEST!

The magnificent epic series of the brave pioneers who
built a railroad, a nation, and a dream.

*Here is a special excerpt from this unforgettable saga
by Franklin Carter—available from Jove Books . . .*

CHAPTER ONE

Omaha, Nebraska, Early Spring, 1866

Construction Engineer Glenn Gilchrist stood on the melting surface of the frozen Missouri River with his heart hammering his rib cage. Poised before him on the eastern bank of the river was the last Union Pacific supply train asked to make this dangerous river crossing before the ice broke to flood south. The temperatures had soared as an early chinook had swept across the northern plains and now the river's ice was sweating like a fat man in July. A lake of melted ice was growing deeper by the hour and there was still this last critical supply train to bring across.

"This is madness!" Glenn whispered even as the waiting locomotive puffed and banged with impatience while huge crowds from Omaha and Council Bluffs stomped their slushy shorelines to keep their feet warm. Fresh out of the Harvard School of Engineering, Glenn had measured and remeasured the depth and stress-carrying load of the rapidly melting river yet still could not be certain if it would support the tremendous weight of this last supply train. But Union Pacific's vice president, Thomas Durant, had given the bold order that it was to cross, and there were enough fools to be found willing to man the train and its supply cars, so here Glenn was, standing in the middle of the Missouri and about half sure he was about to enter a watery grave.

Suddenly, the locomotive engineer blasted his steam whistle and leaned out his window. "We got a full head of steam and the temperature is risin', Mr. Gilchrist!"

Glenn did not hear the man because he was imagining what would happen the moment the ice broke through. Good Lord, they could all plunge to the bottom of Big Muddy and be swept along under the ice for hundreds of miles to a frozen death. A vision flashed before Glenn's eyes of an immense ragged hole in the ice fed by two sets of rails feeding into the cold darkness of the Missouri River.

The steam whistle blasted again. Glenn took a deep breath, raised his hand, and then chopped it down as if he were swinging an ax. Cheers erupted from both riverbanks and the locomotive jerked tons of rails, wooden ties, and track-laying hardware into motion.

Glenn swore he could feel the weakening ice heave and buckle the exact instant the Manchester locomotive's thirty tons crunched its terrible weight onto the river's surface. Glenn drew in a sharp breath. His eyes squinted into the blinding glare of ice and water as the railroad tracks swam toward the advancing locomotive through melting water. The sun bathed the rippling surface of the Missouri River in a shimmering brilliance. The engineer began to blast his steam whistle and the crowds roared at each other across the frozen expanse. Glenn finally expelled a deep breath, then started to backpedal as he motioned the locomotive forward into railroading history.

Engineer Bill Donovan was grinning like a fool and kept yanking on the whistle cord, egging on the cheering crowds.

"Slow down!" Glenn shouted at the engineer, barely able to hear his own voice as the steam whistle continued its infernal shriek.

But Donovan wasn't about to slow down. His unholy grin was as hard as the screeching iron horse he rode and Glenn could hear Donovan shouting to his firemen to shovel faster. Donovan was pushing him, driving the locomotive ahead as if he were intent on forcing Glenn aside and charging across the river to the other side.

"Slow down!" Glenn shouted, backpedaling furiously.

But Donovan wouldn't pull back on his throttle, which

left Glenn with just two poor choices. He could either leap aside and let the supply train rush past, or he could try to swing on board and wrestle its control from Donovan. It might be the only thing that would keep the ice from swallowing them alive.

Glenn chose the latter. He stepped from between the shivering rails, and when Donovan and his damned locomotive charged past drenching him in a bone-chilling sheet of ice water, Glenn lunged for the platform railing between the cab and the coal tender. The locomotive's momentum catapulted him upward to sprawl between the locomotive and tender.

"Dammit!" he shouted, clambering to his feet. "The ice isn't thick enough to take both the weight and a pounding! You were supposed to . . ."

Glenn's words died in his throat an instant later when the ice cracked like rifle fire and thin, ragged schisms fanned out from both sides of the tracks. At the same time, the rails and the ties they rested upon rolled as if supported by the storm-tossed North Atlantic.

"Jesus Christ!" Donovan shouted, his face draining of color and leaving him ashen. "We're going under!"

"Throttle down!" Glenn yelled as he jumped for the brake.

The locomotive's sudden deceleration threw them both hard against the firebox, searing flesh. The fireman's shovel clattered on the deck as his face corroded with terror and the ice splintered outward from them with dark tentacles.

"Steady!" Glenn ordered, grabbing the young man's arm because he was sure the kid was about to jump from the coal tender. "Steady now!"

The next few minutes were an eternity but the ice held as they crossed the center of the Missouri and rolled slowly toward the Nebraska shore.

"Come on!" a man shouted from Omaha. "Come on!"

Other watchers echoed the cry as the spectators began to take heart.

"We're going to make it, sir!" Donovan breathed, banging Glenn on the shoulder. "Mr. Gilchrist, we're by Gawd goin' to make it!"

"Maybe. But if the ice breaks behind us, the supply cars

will drag us into the river. If that happens, we jump and take our chances."

"Yes, sir!" the big Irishman shouted, his square jaw bumping rapidly up and down.

Donovan reeked of whiskey and his eyes were bright and glassy. Glenn turned to look at the young fireman. "Mr. Chandlis, have you been drinking too?"

"Not a drop, sir." Young Sean Chandlis pointed to shore and cried, "Look, Mr. Gilchrist, we've made it!"

Glenn felt the locomotive bump onto the tracks resting on the solid Nebraska riverbank. Engineer Donovan blasted his steam whistle and nudged the locomotive's throttle causing the big drivers to spin a little as they surged up the riverbank. Those same sixty-inch driving wheels propelled the supply cars into Omaha where they were enfolded by the jubilant crowd.

The scene was one of pandemonia as Donovan kept yanking on his steam whistle and inciting the crowd. Photographers crowded around the locomotive taking pictures.

"Come on and smile!" Donovan shouted in Glenn's ear. "We're heroes!"

Glenn didn't feel like smiling. His knees wanted to buckle from the sheer relief of having this craziness behind him. He wanted to smash Donovan's grinning face for starting across the river too fast and for drinking on duty. But the photographers kept taking pictures and all that Glenn did was to bat Donovan's hand away from the infernal steam whistle before it drove him mad.

God, the warm, fresh chinook winds felt fine on his cheeks and it was good to be still alive. Glenn waved to the crowd and his eyes lifted back to the river that he knew would soon be breaking up if this warm weather held. He turned back to gaze westward and up to the city of Omaha. Omaha—when he'd arrived last fall, it had still been little more than a tiny riverfront settlement. Today, it could boast a population of more than six thousand, all anxiously waiting to follow the Union Pacific rails west.

"We did it!" Donovan shouted at the crowd as he raised his fists in victory. "We did it!"

Glenn saw a tall beauty with reddish hair pushing forward

through the crowd, struggling mightily to reach the supply train. "Who is that?"

Donovan followed his eyes. "Why, that's Mrs. Megan Gallagher. Ain't she and her sister somethin', though!"

Glenn had not even noticed the smaller woman with two freckled children in tow who was also waving to the train and trying to follow her sister to its side. Glenn's brow furrowed. "Are their husbands on this supply train?"

Donovan's wide grin dissolved. "Well, Mr. Gilchrist, I know you told everyone that only single men could take this last one across, but . . ."

Glenn clenched his fists in surprise and anger. "Donovan, don't you understand that the Union Pacific made it clear that there was to be no drinking and no married men on this last run! Dammit, you broke both rules! I've got no choice but to fire all three of you."

"But, sir!"

Glenn felt sick at heart but also betrayed. Bill "Wild Man" Donovan was probably the best engineer on the payroll but he'd proved he was also an irresponsible fool, one who played to the crowd and was more than willing to take chances with other men's lives and the Union Pacific's rolling stock and precious construction supplies.

"I'm sorry, Donovan. Collect your pay from the paymaster before quitting time," Glenn said, swinging down from the cab into the pressing crowd. Standing six feet three inches, Glenn was tall enough to look over the sea of humanity and note that Megan Gallagher and her sister were embracing their triumphant husbands. It made Glenn feel even worse to think that those two men would be without jobs before this day was ended.

Men pounded Glenn on the back in congratulations but he paid them no mind as he pushed through the crowd, moving off toward the levee where these last few vital tons of rails, ties, and other hardware were being stored until the real work of building a railroad finally started.

"Hey!" Donovan shouted, overtaking Glenn and pulling him up short. "You can't fire me! I'm the best damned engineer you've got!"

"*Were* the best," Glenn said, tearing his arm free, "now step aside."

But Donovan didn't budge. The crowd pushed around the two large men, clearly puzzled as to the matter of this dispute in the wake of such a bold and daring success only moments earlier.

"What'd he do wrong?" a man dressed in a tailored suit asked in a belligerent voice. "By God, Bill Donovan brought that train across the river and that makes him a hero in my book!"

This assessment was loudly applauded by others. Glenn could feel resentment building against him as the news of his decision to fire three of the crew swept through the crowd. "This is a company matter. I don't make the rules, I just make sure that they are followed."

Donovan chose to appeal to the crowd. "Now you hear that, folks. Mr. Gilchrist is going to fire three good men without so much as a word of thanks. And that's what the working man gets from this railroad for risking his life!"

"Drop it," Glenn told the big Irishman. "There's nothing left to be gained from this."

"Isn't there?"

"No."

"You're making a mistake," Donovan said, playing to the crowd. The confident Irishman thrust his hand out with a grin. "So why don't we let bygones be bygones and go have a couple of drinks to celebrate? Gallagher and Fox are two of the best men on the payroll. They deserve a second chance. Think about the fact they got wives and children."

Glenn shifted uneasily. "I'll talk to Fox and Gallagher but you were in charge and I hold you responsible."

"Hell, we made it in grand style, didn't we!"

"Barely," Glenn said, "and you needlessly jeopardized the crew and the company's assets, that's why you're still fired."

Donovan flushed with anger. "You're a hard, unforgiving man, Gilchrist."

"And you are a fool when you drink whiskey. Later, I'll hear Fox's and Gallagher's excuses."

"They drew lots for a cash bonus ride across that damned

melting river!" Donovan swore, his voice hardening. "Gallagher and Fox needed the money!"

"The Union Pacific didn't offer any bonus! It was your job to ask for volunteers and choose the best to step forward."

Donovan shrugged. He had a lantern jaw, and heavy, fist-scarred brows overhanging a pair of now very angry and bloodshot eyes. "The boys each pitched in a couple dollars into a pot. I'll admit it was my idea. But the winners stood to earn fifty dollars each when we crossed."

"To leave wives and children without support?" Glenn snapped. "That's a damned slim legacy."

"These are damned slim times," Donovan said. "The idea was, if we drowned, the money would be used for the biggest funeral and wake Omaha will ever see. And if we made it . . . well, you saw the crowd."

"Yeah," Glen said. "If you won, you'd flood the saloons and drink it up so either way all the money would go for whiskey."

"Some to the wives and children," Donovan said quietly.

"Like hell."

Glenn started to turn and leave the man but Donovan's voice stopped him cold. "If you turn away, I'll drop you," the Irishman warned in a soft, all the more threatening voice.

"That would be a real mistake," Glenn said.

Although several inches taller than the engineer, Glenn had no illusions as to matching the Irishman's strength or fighting ability. Donovan was built like a tree stump and was reputed to be one of the most vicious brawlers in Omaha. If Glenn had any advantage, it was that he had been on Harvard's collegiate boxing club and gained some recognition for quickness and a devastating left hook that had surprised and then floored many an opponent.

"Come on, sir," Donovan said with a friendly wink as he reached into his coat pocket and dragged out a pint of whiskey. The engineer uncorked and extended it toward Glenn. "So I got a little carried away out there. No harm, was there?"

"I'm sorry," Glenn said, pivoting around on his heel and starting off toward the levee to oversee the stockpiling and handling of this last vital shipment.

This time when Donovan's powerful fingers dug into Glenn's shoulder to spin him around, Glenn dropped into a slight crouch, whirled, and drove his left hook upward with every ounce of power he could muster. The punch caught Donovan in the gut. The big Irishman's cheeks blew out and his eyes bugged. Glenn pounded him again in the solar plexus and Donovan staggered, his face turning fish-belly white. Glenn rocked back and threw a textbook combination of punches to the bigger man's face that split Donovan's cheek to the bone and dropped him to his knees.

"You'd better finish me!" Donovan gasped. " 'Cause I swear to settle this score!"

Glenn did not take the man's threat lightly. He cocked back his fist but he couldn't deliver the knockout blow, not while the engineer was gasping in agony. "Stay away from me," Glenn warned before he hurried away.

He felt physically and emotionally drained by the perilous river crossing and his fight with Donovan. He had been extremely fortunate to survive both confrontations. It had reinforced the idea in his mind that he was not seasoned enough to be making such critical decisions. It wasn't that he didn't welcome responsibility, for he did. But not so much and not so soon.

The trouble was that the fledgling Union Pacific itself was in over its head. No one knew from one day to the next whether it would still be in operation or who was actually in charge. From inception, Vice President Thomas Durant, a medical doctor turned railroad entrepreneur, was the driving force behind getting the United States Congress to pass two Pacific Railway Acts through Congress. With the Civil War just ending and the nation still numb from the shock of losing President Abraham Lincoln, the long discussed hope of constructing a transcontinental railroad was facing tough sledding. Durant himself was sort of an enigma, a schemer and dreamer whom some claimed was a charlatan while others thought he possessed a brilliant organizational mind.

Glenn didn't know what to think of Durant. It had been through him that he'd landed this job fresh out of engineering school as his reward for being his class valedictorian. So far,

Glenn's Omaha experience had been nothing short of chaotic. Lacking sufficient funds and with the mercurial Durant dashing back and forth to Washington, there had been a clear lack of order and leadership. It had been almost three years since Congress had agreed to pay both the Union Pacific and the Central Pacific Railroads the sums of $16,000 per mile for track laid over the plains, $32,000 a mile through the arid wastes of the Great Basin, and a whopping $48,000 per mile for track laid over the Rocky and the Sierra Nevada mountain ranges.

Now, with the approach of spring, the stage had been set to finally begin the transcontinental race. One hundred miles of roadbed had been graded westward from Omaha and almost forty miles of temporary track had been laid. For two years, big paddlewheel steamboats had been carrying mountains of supplies up the Missouri River. There were three entire locomotives still packed in shipping crates resting on the levee while two more stood assembled beside the Union Pacific's massive new brick roundhouse with its ten locomotive repair pits. Dozens of hastily constructed shops and offices surrounded the new freight and switching yards.

There was still more work than men and that was a blessing for veterans in the aftermath of the Civil War joblessness and destruction. Every day, dozens more ex-soldiers and fortune seekers crossed the Missouri River into Omaha and signed on with the Union Pacific Railroad. Half a nation away, the Central Pacific Railroad was already attacking the Sierra Nevada Mountains but Glenn had heard that they were not so fortunate in hiring men because of the stiff competition from the rich gold and silver mines on the Comstock Lode.

Glenn decided he would have a few drinks along with some of the other officers of the railroad, then retire early. He was dog-tired and the strain of these last few days of worrying about the stress-carrying capacity of the melting ice had enervated him to the point of bone weariness.

Glenn realized he would be more than glad when the generals finally arrived to take command of the Union Pacific. He would be even happier when the race west finally began in dead earnest.

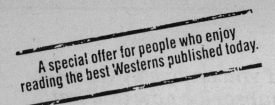

A special offer for people who enjoy reading the best Westerns published today.

WESTERNS!

NO OBLIGATION

Mail the coupon below

To start your subscription and receive 2 FREE WESTERNS, fill out the coupon below and mail it today. We'll send your first shipment which includes 2 FREE BOOKS as soon as we receive it.

Mail To: **True Value Home Subscription Services, Inc. P.O. Box 5235**
120 Brighton Road, Clifton, New Jersey 07015-5235

YES! I want to start reviewing the very best Westerns being published today. Send me my first shipment of 6 Westerns for me to preview FREE for 10 days. If I decide to keep them, I'll pay for just 4 of the books at the low subscriber price of $2.75 each; a total $11.00 (a $21.00 value). Then each month I'll receive the 6 newest and best Westerns to preview Free for 10 days. If I'm not satisfied I may return them within 10 days and owe nothing. Otherwise I'll be billed at the special low subscriber rate of $2.75 each; a total of $16.50 (at least a $21.00 value) and save $4.50 off the publishers price. There are never any shipping, handling or other hidden charges. I understand I am under no obligation to purchase any number of books and I can cancel my subscription at any time, no questions asked. In any case the 2 FREE books are mine to keep.

Name _____

Street Address _____ Apt. No. _____

City _____ State _____ Zip Code _____

Telephone _____

Signature _____
(if under 18 parent or guardian must sign)

Terms and prices subject to change. Orders subject
to acceptance by True Value Home Subscription
Services, Inc.

899